I0618758

THE EXPANSION BOOK 2
CONTACT

DEVON C. FORD

PRESS

PRESS

First published by DHP Publishing in 2018
Published by Vulpine Press in the United Kingdom in 2020

Cover image by Jamie Glover at www.eruleanfuture.com
Cover by Claire Wood

ISBN: 978-1-83919-333-0

www.vulpine-press.com

"Two possibilities exist: Either we are alone in the Universe or we are not. Both are equally terrifying."

Arthur C. Clarke

PROLOGUE

Proxima Centauri B

The four armored shapes walked slowly, tactically. They had left the noisy landing site under the guard of three other armored soldiers and advanced as though patrolling a potentially hostile environment, but they would have been fools not to consider hostility to be a permanent threat where they were.

The one in the lead, moving as stealthily as one of the big cats that lived on their home world, crept slowly towards the source of the signal they had detected. That world was trillions of kilometers away. It would take years to reach their home world were it not for the revolutionary new technology that had brought them here. Now they had the ability to reach beyond their own solar system, to actually travel to places where otherwise only the most powerful of deep space telescopes could see. Now they could go to the dull, red star that bathed their environment in a dark light, and cast eerie and unnatural shadows.

Those telescopes had surmised that there was a planet there, and even guessed its size. After waiting for the suspected planet to cross between Earth and the small red dwarf star, its circumference could be measured and calculated against the passage of time.

Well, that planet was no longer a theory to them; it was no longer a speck of black silhouetted against the red glow but was real dirt beneath their feet. The scientists had gone crazy at the first scans of

1

the exoplanet carried out by their unmanned drones, and Kyle Torres, the unexpected captain of their ship, had to remind them of protocol. They were expected to put their safety and the mission above scientific discovery.

He had enough nightmares about alien DNA infecting them from watching movies, but when faced with the slightest possibility that this unseen world could harm them, he had become almost paranoid about the risks.

The soldier on point stopped; the sudden lack of careful movement resonated as a movement in itself, such was the smooth fluidity of his precise steps. He held his right hand up in a fist, his left still firmly holding the grip of the prototype bullpup carbine he carried in the high ready position. The three others froze similarly until he gave further instructions. None of them was so inexperienced as to ask what he had seen. They merely waited silently and dialed in their senses.

The figure nearest him in their spread-out configuration held her body still as her eyes scanned everything in her field of vision. Her HUD, flashing insanely on the inside of her visor, annoyed her as it worked overtime to identify the new structures of trees and leaves it registered. She had yet to find a way to disable the function with the interactive menus at her disposal. Everything that couldn't be identified was highlighted and logged for analysis as a potential threat, and since they were the first humans ever to set foot on the alien planet orbiting this very strange kind of sun, everything her suit tried to identify existed in no database she could access. Her equipment registered *everything* as possibly dangerous.

The raised fist ahead of her split into four fingers and a thumb spread wide and her body moved on instinct. The servos of her powered armor responded in a fraction of a second, which most of the time wasn't noticeable. But when her lead soldier had given the signal for them to disperse, her body had released adrenaline into her bloodstream and heightened every sense at her disposal to make even the smallest of reactionary delays apparent.

They dispersed, dropping low and taking whatever small cover they could find with no advanced warning. They trained their guns ahead of them to wait for either the all-clear or until whatever had spooked their pet ghost, their Specter, came out fighting.

Long seconds ticked by until she couldn't bear the inactivity any longer. Nothing showed on her suit's HUD. Whatever he had seen or heard was imperceptible to her. Commander Leslie Brandt was not a woman taken to flights of fancy or possessing a superstitious mentality, but she had an ominously bad feeling creeping up from the pit of her stomach.

"Specter," she whispered into the helmet, knowing that her voice would be carried over their wireless connection to play in perfect clarity for him. "What's the deal?"

Specter, the man who had once been the commander's friend and fellow United Nations Peacekeeper but who was now cybernetically rebuilt, answered her. She had learned over the last few weeks not to call him by the name she had known him as, but that self-enforced distance didn't stop his words from chilling her skin and making the tiny hairs stand up, His response prompted an involuntary shudder that she tried to control.

"There's something here, Commander," he said. "It isn't registering on the HUD, but there is something nearby. Something alive."

"How do you know?" came the sweet but steely voice of the other female on the team, Amare Eze.

"Because I think I'm looking at it," Specter answered icily, "and I think it's looking straight at me."

"What can you see?" Brandt whispered as she fought to control her tensed muscles. She was painfully aware that the cover she was behind—a small tree with black, moist bark—was just cover from view. It wouldn't protect her from any dangerous projectiles. Her mind flew off on a wild tangent, wondering if whatever alien was stalking them could camouflage itself and if it would have weaponry capable of carving through the wood and her armor behind it.

"Humanoid, tall," Specter said softly, his body unmoving. "Large eyes."

"Increase optical wavelength," Eze's voice said from behind and to her right. "Turn it right down to the end of the visible light spectrum."

"It's already dialed down to red light spectrum," Brandt answered.

"I know, mine too. Just… just wiggle it around a little," Eze told her.

Brandt did so, scrolling through the menu with her eyes and activating the controls she needed without moving her body to twitch the spectrum up and down. The slight change in the depth of the shadows gave away her adjustment, and in that bending light she saw the faint outline of what Specter had seen.

Thin limbs that seemed insufficient to support the weight of the large head that bore big, black elliptical eyes. She gasped, her brain registering the actual proof of the existence of alien life standing thirty paces from her.

It turned its head, looking directly at her.

No way it could have heard me, she thought. *My suit is sealed.* The figure cocked its head, very slowly, as if regarding her before taking

4

any action. Brandt's fingers tightened involuntarily on the grip of her weapon. As if sensing the fear-induced threat of violence, the alien recoiled and moved backwards fast into shadow as a series of croaks and rattling clicks sounded in their ears. Brandt's suit software tried to recognize the sound as a form of spoken communication and gave her a waiting icon as it tried to decipher and translate it.

"Wait!" Eze called aloud, making all of them freeze momentarily. "It is not hostile. It's... it's *scared*."

Scared of what? Brandt thought with shock. *Oh, right. Us. The armed aliens.*

"It's alright," Specter said aloud, surprising them all as he stepped out into the open with slung weapons to show empty hands.

"Specter," Brandt hissed. "Stand down!"

"It's okay, Commander," he said confidently. "It doesn't want to hurt us."

"He's right," Eze said from behind her as she too stepped out of cover. "It needs our help."

Brandt lowered her weapon, flipping the carbine onto her back where it magnetically locked into place. She was overcome with an unnaturally sudden sense of reassurance and calm. She stepped into the open, joining Specter and Eze in a line as the shadows in the dull, low red glow ahead of them moved and morphed into the tall, big-eyed alien that stood a full head higher than them.

Not understanding why, they each felt a new sensation: relief.

And hope.

CHAPTER 1

UN American Territory HQ, NYC, Earth

"It's unfortunate, Commander," one of the two UNID men said without conviction.

"Unfortunate?" the other man asked dangerously, turning halfway and eyeing the man who had spoken. "It's more than *unfortunate,* it's… it's *mutiny.* That's what it is. These brigands you left in charge of my ship have stolen it. Taken it without permission. They are *pirates!*"

"Sir," the other suited man crooned placatingly, "the main event is yet to happen, as you know. The colony ships are progressing far ahead of schedule, and as there will be a small fleet, the senior commander would be named admiral."

At the mention of the elevation in rank, the man stopped pacing and pricked up his ears. He was short, only slightly below average height but enough to make him self-conscious and defensive. He was irascible and permanently in a foul temper thanks to the stomach cramps that plagued him daily. The commander ran a tight ship, as he liked to claim often and loudly. His strictness meant rigorous discipline and the men and women under his command working to avoid punishment, as opposed to doing their best to please a leader they respected. His style, according to some, served only to make those men and women under his command better at shirking their

6

duties and not getting caught. That said, he was a well-qualified and capable captain.

"An admiralcy, you say?"

The older of the suited men, the one who had introduced himself as Curtis, smiled. He had the man firmly on his hook now. They had been tasked with calming the officer, UNPF commander Wright, who had transferred from the British section of the European territory some years earlier. He had been promoted quickly and sent across the Atlantic with a glowing reference. What soon became obvious to his new hosts was that the praise and promotion had been a clever coup on the part of the Brits, as they had saddled the American UN with a loud, arrogant, yet annoyingly competent senior officer who had dreams of chasing his career further up the ladder. The sheer number of senior commanders who had specialized to command ships in space meant that an admiral's position would be very difficult to attain before the enforced termination of his career after twenty-five years; only those serving longer were the top echelons of the senior ranks.

The task of commanding the colony ships, each with a token frigate escort flanking them, had been an opportunity for the man to gain long-term command experience in deep space. His maneuverings had landed him the job of commanding the *Bōken sha Ichi* on its reconnaissance journey, on *humanity's* first journey, beyond their solar system. The events that unfolded on the surface of the moon two weeks before had thrown all of those well-laid plans well and truly out of the window, and the would-be captain had to face the ignominious return journey after nearly five hours in transit to the moon.

He had been informed of the events unfolding while in flight. He had already been forced to share the ship with a team of brooding

CP men and women lounging around in their armor and not sitting in the regulation allocated berths. Their disregard of protocol annoyed him.

His luggage, all of his books and empty journals that he'd intended to keep in his neat handwriting, all had to be unloaded back on Earth, where he had already given up his accommodation.

Now, after being asked many times over the previous two weeks to wait for further orders, the carrot of overall fleet command dangled in front of him. Or so he thought. Next to Curtis, the younger suited man's comm device bleeped softly, making him turn away slightly to view it. He was unable to mask his face registering a sudden drop and a mischievous smile before Curtis interrupted his thoughts.

"What is it, kid?" he growled, annoyed that the younger man had yet to tell him what had interrupted his conversation. In answer, Ward showed him the message he had just received.

"What is it?" the short commander with dreams of an admiral's wreathed star adorning his chest asked irritably.

"Commander, my superior would like to speak to you," Curtis said as he stood and smoothed down his suit jacket. He turned to open the door, but it swung inward by itself before he could get there, making him jump out of the way of a severe woman with a buzz-cut hairdo. She regarded him briefly, wondering why he stood startled in the middle of the room, and dismissed him instantly.

"Commander Wright?" she asked, not waiting for any response or offering a hand to shake. "My name is Crawford. I'm the section chief in joint command of these missions."

The commander nodded, standing stiffly and finding himself outmatched by her slightly above-average height.

"Commander, I'm not at liberty to discuss the finer points, but what I can say is that the mission parameters have changed. The UNID thanks you for your service, but we will be appointing a different commanding officer from here on and you will be reassigned." She nodded, offered the slightest hint of a smile as though she had seen someone do that once and tried to emulate it, and turned to walk away.

She had made it as far as reaching for the door handle before he found his voice.

"This... this is *preposterous,*" he exploded. "I did not give up my previous command, my quarters, almost all of my possessions simply for the UNI-*bloody*-D to change its mind and cast me aside like some common seaman. I demand to speak to your superiors; perhaps they will see my worth and reward me with command, as they previously promised."

Crawford stopped and turned to face him. Seeing the short bull of a man's chest heaving up and down reminded her of a toddler who was on the verge of throwing the mother of all tantrums.

"Sir," she said, this time with a small smile that was genuine. "Before I respond, might I enquire as to why *you* feel that you're the best qualified and most appropriate officer to command the fleet we aim to send out of the solar system?"

Commander Wright stammered, unable to answer after being put on the spot and covering that uncertainty in himself with bluster.

"Who are you to ask me that?" he said in a voice slightly louder than he intended. "How dare you question my abili—"

"Would you order your ships to fire on other UN vessels, if required, to achieve the mission objectives?" she asked, silencing him. "Would you order the troops put under your command to board a ship and capture or kill the crew to seize control of it? Are you competent enough to strategize battle plans to secure facilities on alien worlds?"

"Why on Earth would I?" he blurted out, his face red with temper and frustration. "What possible circumstances would dictate that I—"

"Sir, very simply put, we feel that you lack the tenacity to get the job done. We have assigned a man who is battle-tested to lead the fleet, and frankly, I believe that to award you a command of one of those ships would jeopardize the mission through your own need to undermine the overall commander."

He stopped his next words before they started to come out of his mouth. That was exactly what he would do, if he was being honest with himself. In an instant of clarity, he knew that what she said was right, but what was more, it would doubtless be backed up by any number of psych-evals and anecdotal evidence. He tried another approach, still desperate to get on the mission and immortalize his name.

"If," he said carefully, "I knew the person you were planning to make admiral, I could give assurances that I would abide by their command unquestioningly."

Crawford seemed to assess him, to weigh up his words to find any hidden agenda in them. In the end, she saw no harm in revealing the identity of their prime candidate to lead the colony fleet to Proxima.

"We have someone in mind," she said just as carefully, "but he has power of veto over all UN personnel listings. It's not me you'd have to convince."

Wright's eyebrows rose to silently ask the question of who exactly he had to blow around there to get a job.

"Commander Dassiova will be promoted to admiral prior to mission launch."

UN Shipbuilding Yards, Earth Orbit

"It's a helluva responsibility, Elias," said the old man dismissively.

His wrinkled face was too close to the viewscreen, as though the previous two decades of having a newer video unit as his home comm device were still a novelty to him. Dassiova fought the urge to tell his father to lean back so he could see him, because he knew he was leaning closer to see the screen where his son was displayed. The stubborn old man, a veteran of the UNPF himself, had refused the laser corrective eye surgery so many times that the healthcare program given to everyone who served simply stopped offering him the option. That meant that every time the dutiful son logged on his weekly call to the old man, he had to suffer a conversation with a close-up of his hairy nostrils and just deal with it.

"Yes, sir, it is," he told his father. "But it's a huge responsibility and it will be a first for mankind."

Dassiova senior gave a gruff grunt of agreement. It was clear that he disapproved simply because it was an idea invented by younger people.

"Plus," Dassiova said, unsure how the old man would respond, "I'll make admiral, they tell me."

A loud barking croak came from the other end of the viewscreen, showing an open mouth with most of the teeth missing, and a curious racking, huffing noise came over the speakers. It was breathless laughter at Elias's expense, which was what he was worried about. His father had served eighteen years, rising to the rank of master petty officer before an injury in training ended his career. He still limped as a result of the poor battlefield surgical care that was offered back then, but returning home to his young son was supposed to be a positive thing for the whole family. When the young Elias Dassiova grew up and left school to join the UNPF, his father had been proud until he realized that his boy had been selected for the Officer Training Academy on his aptitude scores.

Young Ensign Dassiova, sent away to active conflicts still flaring up in the Middle East as soon as he had qualified, spent his graduation ceremony scanning the crowds and wearing his service medals on the breast of his ill-fitting suit. He never saw his father, and part of him hardened that day.

"Yes," he said sternly, "I'll be an admiral. And it's unlikely that I'll be able to check in with you every week. I've organized for the care company to increase their visits while I'm... *away.*"

The old man still laughed, a cruel and derisive laugh at his expense. When so many thousands of men and women would be desperate to gain his attention and approval, this one mean old man held the power of acceptance over him.

"Look after yourself, Dad," he told him. "Do what the nurses say and don't give them any trouble."

"Yes sir, Admiral Eli, sir!" the old man laughed mockingly as his son cut the connection.

He left his private quarters on base, walking the short distance to the mess hall. He wore the shirtsleeve-order uniform of the UNPF and similarly dressed young men and women stopped in the corridors to snap to attention and salute him as he passed. Dassiova returned the salutes, wishing he could get a moment to breathe. There were so many subordinates crammed into the small complex for build-up training. The privilege of rank and seniority allowed him to take his meals separately, but despite the crammed mess hall, he preferred that the men and women who made up the crew of his fleet saw him eating and training alongside them.

He exchanged nods and greetings, luckily not having to suffer the endless string of salutes—those weren't required in the mess halls or crash decks unless prompted. He took a white tray, sliding it along the rails and picking up the individual portions of food as he listened to the conversations going on around him. He finished with three glasses of fresh orange juice, which clinked together as he looked for a place to sit and eat. Picking an empty gap near a group of young, fit-looking seamen wearing the lightning bolt badges he was looking for, he rested his tray and downed the first glass of juice. He had a vague idea in his head, an idea to put fresh eyes on the problem he had been updated about daily. He felt that a good, old-fashioned in the trenches approach might help, hence his reason for seeking out the electrical engineers.

"I heard it was a deep-space mission," one of them said. "Bull-shit," another countered. "It's a Red Run. Has to be."

"Oh, and you're an expert? How many times you been to Mars, Hunter?"

"Once," Hunter replied quickly. "What's your count, Judge?" He smiled at her sullen silence, as he knew they had only been on the same journey to the red planet and back together.

Dassiova glanced up; the tall young man who had spoken was sporting a petty officer class two rank and eyeballing a young female in the jump suit of an engineer rating. He guessed she was Judge. Her lack of an answer and Hunter's arrogance prompted Dassiova to offer his opinion.

"It's a Red Run," he said quietly, sensing them all turn to see the senior commander sitting beside them as they talked shit about his mission. "At least it is to begin with, and I'd know because I've done seven of them. We may be going a little farther than that, in time."

Silence answered him, either through fear or confusion, he couldn't be sure. He chopped at the thick oatmeal with his spoon before trying some. He turned and looked at them genially, which seemed to only have the effect of scaring them more.

"At ease, kids," he said, hoping to relax them. They all lapsed deeper into the silence as they ate their breakfast.

"Sir?" Dassiova looked up to see Judge looking straight at him. "What is it, Judge?" She colored up involuntarily at his use of her name but held her own.

"What have we got that's farther than Mars?" Dassiova smiled.

"All in good time," he told her. "What's your assignment?"

"We're electrical engineers assigned to the *Venture*, sir," she responded.

"Flagship of the fleet?" Dassiova asked with a smile. "Not a bad gig. You seen her yet?"

Heads shook hesitantly, but only Judge had the strength of character to answer him:

"Negative."

"What are your orders today?" he asked her.

"Training on ship systems," she recited, "and PT."

"Well, you look fit and healthy enough," he told her. "Petty Officer Hunter?"

"…Sir?"

"Seaman Judge is assigned to me for today. Give your officer my compliments that I'll be borrowing her."

14

CHAPTER 2

Deep Space Near Proxima Centauri

"Good morning everyone," Captain Torres said as he took his seat from a grateful bridge officer who had occupied it for the night shift. "Tactical? Sitrep please."

"Morning, sir," the crewman at the tactical station responded. "We currently have eighty percent of our recon drones in the water. All are reporting functional and feeding telemetry back to the mainframe."

"Any signal contacts?"

"Negative, sir," the comm operator responded. "Cyclic scanning of all frequencies shows both high and low frequency waves, but they appear to be just bouncing around. Nothing seems to be aimed at us and nothing bears any recognizable language."

"I trust we're recording it all for analysis back home?"

"Affirmative, sir."

"Good," Torres said, pausing to take a sip of coffee. "Commander?" Leslie Brandt turned around in her chair to face the young man who had once been her ensign when she was a lowly petty officer.

"Captain?" she asked him, eying his coffee and wishing she had thought to bring herself a cup.

"What's our state of combat readiness?"

"Always ready, sir," she snapped back, with the earnest tone of an over-eager recruit. "We have a standby team on rotation at all times. I've commandeered a storage area near to the armory for the on-call troops to crash, and Paterson's given us a couple of engineers to work on the gun automation links."

That last fact was helpful, as the four devastatingly powerful and accurate quad minigun emplacements were being accessed by a few key personnel. They were able to remotely activate and operate the guns using the links through their armor's interactive display; like a kind of virtual reality video game with real life stakes.

"That's good," Torres said as he tapped at the display screen built into the arm on his captain's chair. He turned his attention back to the task in hand.

"Tactical, what's the run time on this line?" he asked. Long-lining—the process of dropping reconnaissance drones in space, then returning for them to dock back to their ship to download data and recharge—came from an ancient Earth practice. Humans would take a boat out into rough sea and literally dropping a long fishing line into the waves. The line would have hooks all along it, then the fishermen would wait before going back and dragging on board all the fish that had taken the bait.

It had been banned in the Americas for humanitarian reasons—so many of the large ocean predators the practice killed were endangered. But the theory had curiously lived on in space exploration.

They had reached the end of their line of drones, always maintaining a certain percentage on board in case of losses, and Torres gave the orders to bring them about. They were to plot a jump course for the start of their line.

Even though the co-ordinates were a sure thing, their jumps were still out by a random factor, putting them anywhere between five thousand and fifteen thousand kilometers away from their intended destination.

Paterson had been working on that around the clock for the first few days before he fell asleep in a senior officer's briefing and Torres ordered him to get some rack time. In spite of this effort, he was still no closer to figuring out why their jumps never took them to the precise place they wanted to be. Instead, they stayed well back from the safety line and never plotted a jump near any planetary bodies.

Just in case.

"All set, Captain," Rogers said from the helm.

"Punch it." Brandt felt a lurch in her stomach, like a sudden but fleeting sensation of weightlessness. It disappeared almost the same second it assailed her. As many refinements as Paterson made to the jump process when the Fold Drive engaged, she still felt it and was still left slightly disorientated after they re-emerged into normal space. The shield harmonics matched that of the Fold Drive's magnetic field emitter perfectly, and Paterson had even experimented with the ship's gravity emitter to increase its power output in the moments before a jump, but it still wasn't seamless.

The scientific facts of their jumps had nagged at her in the night, keeping her awake as she tried to comprehend it all. How could they exist where they were and yet not exist in any place or time that anyone could see them? They simply disappeared from one place and reappeared in another, but remained in existence somewhere in between.

Where did we go? Did we go anywhere? Are we real, or is there another version of us back where we started still?

The tiredness, she realized, had made her questions fall off the edge into partial insanity.

Jolted back to the moment as they dropped out of the artificially created wormhole, she mentally steadied herself and glanced down at the screen to the right of her chair.

"Marker detected off our stern, Captain," the technical officer said. "We've overshot it by... eight thousand clicks."

"Bring us about," Torres said. "Start reeling them in. Mister Sarvanto, you have the bridge." He stood, indicating to Brandt with a twitch of his head that she should accompany him. He scanned the UN Intelligence Directorate bio-implant in his left forearm over the reader to open the door to the secure commlink room.

He sat, inputting the authorization codes to start the tiny Fold Drive emitter. This array served as their sub-space communication and allowed them to contact Earth without waiting the forty or so years a message would normally take them. They waited as the call went unanswered, each growing slightly nervous before the screen blinked to life with a dull beep and a suited woman with short hair sat down to face them.

"Captain Torres, Commander Brandt," she said formally, "my name is Crawford."

"Hi," Torres said for want of a more constructive response. He detected no rank by which to address her, and he didn't think she looked like a 'Ma'am' despite evidently being in a position of authority. He had spent enough time in the company of spooks to recognize one, and he was pretty sure he recognized this particular shady UNID agent.

"Allow me to bring you up to speed with what has been going on," Crawford said. "As I'm sure you're aware, you and the entire crew have been disavowed and are speculated to be operating independently of any territory. Obviously, if and when you return with positive results that will have a constructive bearing on human technological advancement, then the true story can emerge in part, and over time, of course." She paused, allowing both Torres and Brandt to fully consider the words she had used. "How far into the reconnaissance of the system are you?"

"We've mapped almost ten percent so far," Torres said, "and we've yet to get close to the nearest exoplanet. But our scans indicated nothing of interest there unless we go in for a closer look. By my best guess, we'll be approaching it within a week, then we can jump ahead a couple light years to investigate the twin suns and any planets orbiting them."

"That's good," Crawford said. "Following that, we will need you to complete the recon of the primary areas of interest in the system and get sample readings from every moon and planetoid along the way."

"Crawford?" Torres asked politely. "Mind if I ask again what our primary goal is? Are we searching for intelligent life, resources or are we homesteading?"

"You're observing, analyzing and reporting back, Captain," Crawford told him with a hint of sternness in her words. Her expression said, 'don't ask.' Her face and her tone told him to do his job and leave the bigger-picture thinking to others.

"Understood," Torres said quickly with forced joviality to change the subject. "Stand by to receive the full data on the adjustments to the Fold Drive." He tapped a few commands on the desk display before looking up to see Crawford's eyes glance at the incoming data file.

"All received, Captain," she said. "Anything else?"

"Ma'am, what's the deal with the colony ships? Are they coming here to meet us if we find somewhere suitable or are they coming regardless?"

"Undetermined," Crawford told him. "Crawford out."

The screen went black and the two old friends were left to sit in silence together.

"She look familiar to you?" Brandt asked.

"You think there's *two* women in UNID who wear guys' suits and get away with a recruit haircut? She debriefed us after the terrorist attack on the moon. I'm guessing she's had a few promotions since then."

"Not just me thinking it, then," Brandt said.

"Thinking what? Like we're still being used and not told the full story?"

"S.O.P., Torres. S.O.P."

Standard operating procedures is about right, Torres told himself.

He forced himself to shake it off and get the job done. The two went back onto the bridge, Sarvanto standing up to vacate the captain's chair as soon as Torres stepped through the door.

"What's our progress time?" he asked.

"Eleven hours to completion, Captain," the tactical officer replied. "Accelerating to maximum sub-light speed in between drones has taken about nine hours off the total time."

That was better. Torres had been annoyed that they were in an uncharted system with the fastest ship known to humanity, but they were curb-crawling to pick up their little sensor drones. Instead, they could have been blasting ahead to find alien life and fascinating new elements not known in their own periodical table.

Within an hour, while enduring the ship's stop and start moves, the tactical officer called out a warning.

"Direct off our port bow," he said rapidly in a voice that held back his panic. "Asteroid storm by the look of it. Multiple small contacts on a collision course."

"Can we accelerate out of the path?" Torres asked.

A pause answered him as everyone onboard waited. "Negative—at least I don't think so…"

"We don't pay for guesses," Torres said. "Helm? Plot us a micro-jump to avoid the asteroids. Eighty thousand kilometers… pu—"

"Sir!" barked the tactical officer. "The asteroids have changed course. They are now veering away ahead of us. No collision warning. They're… they're *accelerating*…"

"All stop," Torres ordered.

"Even *I* know that asteroids don't do that," Brandt said from beside him.

"Scan them," he said. "All frequencies and record for playback."

"Aye, aye, sir," came the response from the comm officer. "Send out our greeting message while you're at it," he said, leaning back to watch the few contacts on his display blinking as they disappeared out of their sensor range.

~

"So, what else happened today? Anything exciting?" Eze asked Brandt as they sat to eat rehydrated protein muesli, which swelled and expanded in response to the water they had added to it. It wasn't exactly a medium-well sirloin, but it was still marginally better than the tablet form of rations they had endured enough times to loathe them.

"Other than some UFO action?" Brandt asked with her eyebrows raised. "I'd say that's pretty frikkin' exciting."

"Unconfirmed," Eze said through her mouthful with a dismissive wave of her plastic spork. "When you send me a picture of you pounding it out with a little green man and throwing up some peace signs, *then* I will subscribe to your alien beliefs."

"We know they're out there," Brandt argued. "It's a scientific impossibility that us dumb monkeys are the only intelligent form of life in the galaxy..." Her words trailed away as the scowling face of Ryan Levenstein eyed them on his way past.

"Speaking of little green men..." Eze said, prompting an unprofessional snort of laughter from the commander at his expense. He was a bureaucrat, a penny-pincher, a corporate bottom-liner who had found himself swept along on the journey. He should count himself lucky. He could have been detained and tortured at some off-grid facility that all the potentially hostile territories would deny controlling. He showed no gratitude for his rescue, however, nor did he seem to appreciate the fact that the crew who had kept him alive on three different occasions now were anything other than lowly employees to him. True, some of the crew and half of the scientists onboard were Hyper.

They worked for the Hudson-Yu Progression and Research company—hence their somewhat sensationalist moniker—but that didn't mean he owned anyone. He had tried to order Torres to turn the ship around and surrender, but the captain's response had been to sever his access to anywhere on the ship that was sensitive and treat him like the civilian observer he was.

No doubt that would bite Torres on the ass at some point, but if they brought back proof of alien life and samples from mineral-rich worlds, then it was doubtful that Levenstein could do a damned thing to any of them.

The two women finished their stiff meal and washed it down with more water from the ship's reclamation system. It was crisp, clear and cold. Nobody would have ever thought it had been distilled from the waste products of the human crew. Their armor suits, even the new and much-improved ones, never quite got the taste right. They returned to the crew quarters they shared to get some sleep as the *Ichi* continued leap-frogging ahead to retrieve the survey drones left floating in space until their automated docking command was activated by the presence of the mothership.

Transmitting out from the ship, radiating away in a repeating pattern of data-burst transmissions and voice over medium and long wave frequencies, their message of peace broadcast out to the new system they flew through.

"We are the crew of the *Bōken Sha*. We are from Earth, a planet in the nearest solar system. We mean no harm, and we come in peace."

Images of their planet, their solar system, of the colonies on the surface of the moon and the first domes created on Mars flashed in rapid sequence to allow anyone receiving their message to see a flip-book history of the evolution of their species. It was all the intel an enemy would need to learn about their species.

CHAPTER 3

UN Shipbuilding Yards, Earth Orbit

"You said you haven't seen her," Dassiova said to his young and somewhat confused shadow as the elevator descended thirty levels to the huge shipbuilding bay. "Here she is."

Seaman Carla Judge stared out of the glass front of the wide elevator and marveled at the sheer gargantuan size of the *Venture*. She was the flagship of a very small colony recon fleet. Most people working on the final stages of her construction didn't know that was her official designation, but they knew that the massive cargo bays and thousands of crew berths meant that the *Venture* wasn't designed to run orbital defense.

"What do you know about her?" Dassiova asked the electrical engineer.

"Fourteen decks," she recited woodenly. "Eighteen separate singularity reactors powering over a hundred main propulsion and repulser maneuvering thrusters. Crew of over six thousand and almost half a mile from bow to stern."

"That's the brochure covered," Dassiova said in mild mockery. He had chilled out considerably after he had accepted the UNID tasking and finally given up command of his fighting unit. It was as though a fatalistic air had fallen over him and he woke each morning just a little less angry at life.

The UN chiefs had tried for years to entice him away from the front line. He had been offered early retirement, half a dozen promotions to take over command of some training compound or other, and even turned down a position at GloCon—the UNID's global control section running the CP teams of SpecOps soldiers dotted all over the territories.

The one show that had enticed him away from the front line, where he probably had expected to die years before, was this. Dassiova was initially offered command of all ground troops destined for a mission out of the system, and when he asked how that was possible, the UNID operatives had extracted a solemn oath—backed up with a promise of life imprisonment somewhere off-world—for his mouth to stay firmly shut. Lawyers were enlisted. NDAs were signed with the full power of a treason charge behind any breach. They had told him about the existence of a device they called a Fold Drive, and how a recon mission was planned to reach the Centauri system with its multiple suns. He had asked how he fitted in with that mission brief, and when they told him about the colony fleet that would be following and that they needed an overall ground commander, he had been unable to resist.

It wasn't the excitement of exploration that drew him, but the whisper of danger posed by an enemy they had yet to meet.

He had accepted that mission, requested a long list of personnel who he had worked with previously—mostly officers who could be trusted to pick their men and women sensibly— and devised a training schedule to ensure that all of the troops under his command were performing at their absolute peak.

But then the mission had gone wrong.

The recon mission that was due to depart about a week prior was way ahead of schedule because, somehow, other territories had heard of the technology they possessed. It was an easy guess that they wanted it for themselves.

There had been a brief engagement between their own UNID and the Hyper mercenaries attached to them against some half-trained unit from a backwater territory. That unit's only tactic was to fire in the general direction of an enemy on full auto until they all ran out of bullets. Dassiova wasn't surprised that the regular troops had received their asses back gift wrapped, because he and a dozen hand-picked men and women could decimate a force three times their number with ease.

It was a simple matter of training, resolve, and sheer ruthlessness.

That recon mission had been forced into action well ahead of time, and the experienced man sent to captain the ship had returned to Earth almost purple with anger. Dassiova knew a few of the CP troops who had been sharing the dropship with the guy and nodded at them with subtle familiarity. If they were sending this particular team, then they were expecting trouble in heavy calibers.

Instead of the experienced captain, who expected to go back out as an admiral, an up-and-coming young officer who had once been an ensign commanded the recon mission. Dassiova wouldn't have remembered the kid if his mom hadn't been an admiral. Plus, the kid had been up close and personal with a terror attack on the moon a few years back under Dassiova's command. That was hard to forget.

And it got worse.

The CP teams sent to run security for the mission were stranded, either on the lunar surface or elsewhere in transit with the captain, when they had to bolt following the compromise.

Now their senior soldier in charge was, remarkably, another one of Dassiova's former troops who had been involved in the same terrorist attack. This one had risen from petty officer to commander courtesy of the fast-track program.

Whatever screw-ups were running the show in the next system over, they had better get results as far as Dassiova was concerned. Results could wash away a lot of bad decisions and failures, because people tended to get excited about the new shiny outcome and not stop to consider whether it was luck or meticulous and ruthless execution of well-made plans that brought home the bacon.

He cast those thoughts aside as the elevator neared the lower level and switched to traveling horizontally along an observation tunnel. They moved toward the nose end of the massive ship where the bridge was located.

He considered the magnitude of his task as he watched the awestruck young woman staring at the flying city he would command in space. There were two of those ships and a dozen others of varying smaller shapes and designs. All of those souls onboard would live or die at his command. Over fifteen thousand lives would be in his hands, and for the first time in his life he wondered if the unbreakable Commander Elias Dassiova was capable of becoming *Admiral* Dassiova. He searched himself and asked the question.

Am I good enough to do this?

"So, what do you know about shield harmonics?" he asked Judge as their lateral elevator car slowed when it neared the walkway leading to the huge hull.

"Err ... they resonate, sir," she said, unsure what the question really meant.

"And you understand how to adjust that resonating frequency? Like flying a shielded ship through another shield?"

"Yes, sir," she responded dutifully. "The only problem is knowing the exact frequency of that shield, obviously."

"Obviously," Dassiova agreed. "So you could match a shield frequency to any harmonic pattern you were given? Is that the case for all of you sparkies?"

She smiled at the UNPF slang for the electrical engineers being used by a senior officer.

"No, sir," she said with a self-deprecating shrug. "I'm just good at it is all."

"Break it down for me," he told her. "Assume I'm taking a harmonic resonance matching class for dummies or something."

Judge thought about it for a moment.

"Well, sir, it's like teaching two kids to harmonize in the school choir, only both of them can't hear for shit so they can't match pitch with anyone else. You need to get one on key, then tell the other to go up or down to be just right along with the first one. If the first one wobbles, the second one can't change so they clash, unless you're on them with the adjustments in time." She blushed slightly at her explanation, worried that she had overstepped.

"I like that analogy." Dassiova said simply as the elevator stopped. He drew back the almost irrelevant safety gate before stepping onto the gangway to board the *Venture*. "Don't look out if you don't have a head for heights." He waved his right hand towards the shielded entrance to the shipyard bay without looking.

Judge made the stomach-flipping error of looking directly out at the edge of Earth juxtaposed against the huge expanse of back void beyond. She almost lost her footing with the sudden disorientation but steadied herself and stepped onto the flagship. Her chest heaved a little, her breaths heavy in reaction to the sudden vertigo. He had been right. She should not have looked down on her home planet to be gripped by the feeling of an imminent and unavoidable fall.

Dassiova watched her with a small smile at the rookie mistake she had made.

"You been at sea much?" he asked her, using the old-school terminology for missions in space.

"One Red Run and the moon twice," she said. "One short tour to do some emergency shield dome maintenance and a vacation with my parents right after I finished high school."

"Last family trip before you joined up, huh?"

"Something like that, sir," Judge replied.

They stopped at an airlock door, which was overridden to be open on both sides but guarded by two UNPF soldiers in the old-style powered armor. One of them recognized Dassiova, greeting him by name and respectfully directing him to log in his visit to the colony ship. Every person who stepped aboard was logged and recorded, giving their reason for being there, even if it was their job to build the engines or decorate the crew quarters. He logged his bio-signature with a scanned handprint and invited Judge to do the same. The terminal prompted her for a reason to board; she wasn't on the ship's pre-approved list.

"Hit *other*," the commander told her, "and use my name as the reason."

She did, nodding to him as she did so, and he set off inside the ship with her in tow. They walked through corridors barely wide enough for two people to cross if their paths clashed, making them do the curious dance where they turned half sideways and shuffled past anyone coming the other way.

Eventually they reached another door on that deck and found it similarly guarded. No data terminal recorded their presence there, and the two guards wore the newer armor Judge had yet to lay eyes on. They opened the door after a nod from Dassiova, who they recognized, and Judge followed him inside.

"You know what that is?" he asked her over the sound of machinery, pointing at a massive conical device.

"Shield generator," she replied in a voice loud enough to cut over the competing sound. "*Big* one."

"And that?" he asked, pointing at a circular control board. It stood vertically and led into a long spike that diminished in width as it extended forward to the prow of the massive ship.

She looked at it, trying to work out what it was.

"No idea, sir," she said simply. "Sorry."

"Don't apologize, Judge," Dassiova told her with none of the scorn or mild antipathy he used to feel for junior enlisted ranks. "I'd rather more people were straight with me instead of making shit up. Most people have never seen one because they're prototypes."

"Prototypes of what?" she asked, her confusion at the surrealism dropping her ingrained manners for her.

"Something that will take us a *looooong* way," Dassiova said wistfully, drawing out the word. He reached out to touch the massive device almost tenderly.

Judge said nothing as she tried to figure out the configuration of the circuit panel in front of her.

"I've got a team of almost thirty scientists trying to figure out how to make this—" he pointed at the unknown device "— talk to this and agree on the tune they want to sing. None of them explained it to me in the way that you just did, which makes me suspicious that they're all eggheads without the ability to roll up their sleeves and get the job done."

Judge thought about it for a while before she spoke.

"I can do it," she told him. No arrogance, no prideful boasting, just confidence in ability.

"Good," Dassiova said again. "Aren't you going to ask what it is?"

Judge shrugged in response. "Figured you'd tell me if you wanted me to know, sir."

"Hypothesize," he told her. He crossed his arms to wait as she chewed her lip slightly and looked away in thought.

"It isn't a shield generator because that's there," she waved behind them, "and it needs to match so whatever it is needs to help the ship pass through something... my guess would be some kind of advanced propulsion system like a constantly accelerating engine they've been talking about for years."

"Think bigger," Dassiova told her quietly.

She fixed him with a look that pleaded to be taken seriously with what was on the tip of her tongue.

"Spit it out, Judge," he growled at her. "Okay, some kind of faster-than-light drive?"

Dassiova's eyebrows went up and his mouth twitched a hint of a smile. Judge's mouth dropped open and her lips formed to say a word she really shouldn't use in front of the man who was about to be the admiral of the fleet.

"*Ffffuuu-orgive* me, sir," she said, demonstrating miraculous poise and recovery, "but why me? Why can't all the eggheads figure it out?"

"I'm sure I don't need to tell you that this is *beyond* classified," he eyeballed her briefly, just long enough to underline his point. "The man who figured it out first did so on the fly in deep space under fire. He was a grunt to begin with—he only became a scientist later—and because he didn't grow up in a lab, he knew how to make

31

it work in the real world and not just on paper. That's why I want fresh eyes on it. *Your* eyes."

She met his intense stare without hesitation. "Yes, sir."

The *Venture* was ready to leave the shipyards three days later. That seventy-two-hour period was filled with the constant rotation of men and women loading the gargantuan vessel with stores day and night.

That forward compartment, the one containing the huge shield array and the prototype device to work in unison with it, remained locked down and guarded throughout every watch by a fresh pair of suited and armed soldiers. Those with clearance came and went un-challenged, as their biometric scans could not be faked. The secrecy surrounding the activities hidden inside the compartment made for ship-wide scuttlebutt before the fleet had even passed the moon.

Two frigates, the *Norton* and the *Hammer*, escorted that fleet, with the *UNS Venture* at its center and the slightly smaller *UNS Cortez* sitting off its starboard flank.

Other smaller ships cross-decked between the bigger vessels al-most constantly. It was mostly the standard dropships that were housed in the enormous flight decks of the two colony ships, but when it came to crunch time, they would have to be sealed up tightly inside one of the motherships or face being left behind in deep space.

All four of the big ships were equipped with a Fold Drive emitter array; the colony ships were built around that technology and the two frigates were retrofitted with the long spike protruding from the nose. In addition, the ships had all of their guns upgraded along with new, more powerful shield emitters. Most of the work had been done as part of a scheduled maintenance haul when both ships had been rotated out of planetary defense roles. This cover prevented any suspicion arising from their sudden disappearance.

The official line for the construction of the colony ships was for a large American territory-led UN mission to Mars. They even went to the trouble of recording news bulletins and interviewing some of the sailors heading to the red planet about their mission. It was all staged, of course, and the people interviewed were probably UNID or else heavily briefed by their officers and NCOs on exactly what they could say.

"Admiral, lunar control wish us a safe journey on to Mars," the comm officer called out.

"Give them our best and my personal thanks," Dassiova responded. He cleared his throat and waited for the courtesy message to be sent. "Give me a fleet-wide channel."

Commands were tapped into the glass interface screen. The young operator nodded to the fleet commander that he was ready to address the almost thirteen thousand souls under his overall command.

"Members of the Ninth Fleet," he began powerfully.

He softened his tone for his next words. "This is Admiral Dassiova onboard the *Venture*. We are now heading for deep space on our way to Mars. As of now there are to be no—I repeat, *no*—comms to anyone not sailing in this fleet. All channels are monitored, and any unauthorized transmissions will result in swift disciplinary action. It is now mission-critical that we go dark." He cleared his throat again as he tried to remember the way he had rehearsed the speech in his large and well-appointed cabins beside the bridge.

"Our mission is much more than the brief you have received, and senior officers were ordered not to disclose this until the fleet was clear from Earth space…" He paused, aware of the gravity of what he was about to say. "Our four main ships are equipped with proto-type devices which will allow us to travel faster than the speed of light. Over the next week we will be testing the final refinements to these devices—these *Fold Drives*—and when we are all fully opera-tional we will be travelling to the Centauri system where an advance recon ship is already in theater."

"Your orders have not changed," he said with an injection of pas-sion. "Do your assigned duties and fulfill your roles well —let's make history. Admiral Dassiova out."

He nodded to the comm officer who cut the transmission, and the admiral let out a breath of pure stress. This was the first time in a career spanning almost twenty years that he felt out of his depth. The first time he felt the stab of nervous apprehension that he was up to the task. He swallowed it down and did what he did best; he drilled his troops well and he kept the momentum and the standards high.

The primary reason for his unease was the sheer scale of his com-mand. He had executive officers for different tasks; the workload managing over twelve thousand UN personnel was high, and he was accustomed to managing only a few hundred at a time. He had to climb the steep learning curve of delegation, and trust in the three other captains to keep their own houses in order and firmly behind his leadership.

As a unit commander on deployment he could engage with every one of his troops, but in charge of just the *Venture* alone he could never hope to visit every deck and every department in less than a week. He had to trust that his senior commanders would pass on his orders and that those orders would be passed on down to each of the crew. He had to trust in the chain of command.

Like it or not, he was the tip of the iceberg and he had to trust that gravity would carry his will down the chain.

"Helm," he said confidently, "take us to flank speed and signal the fleet to match."

CHAPTER 4

Deep Space Near Proxima Centauri

The low, red light bathing the interior of the alien ship cast long shadows that would make any human eyes struggle to make out details. The craft seemed to bear no straight edges; instead it curved everywhere as though it had grown and evolved instead of being constructed. The holo-display set into a rounded plinth in front of a high-backed chair showed the outline of the *Ichi* as it rotated slowly. The image cast off bursts of hieroglyphs as the specifications were analyzed by whatever unknown program deciphered the arrival of the unexpected visitors.

The pilot, doing nothing to actively control the vessel as it traveled slowly on a pre-programmed course, used its slender fingers to tease and manipulate the holographic image of the ship.

A rattling, throaty clicking noise came from behind it in the deeper shadows of the sparsely filled bridge. The pilot turned its large head on a thin neck to look at its companion who had spoken.

It answered, giving a deeper rattle of clicks that rose and fell in tempo and pitch. The response seemed to carry a tone of mild warning or even reprimand. No reply came from the shadows, so the pilot returned to its prodding of the holographic model of the ship.

The clicks sounded again, this time in a tone that seemed almost wistful.

What do you think they want? it asked. *Why have they come here?* The deeper rattle answered.

We do not yet know, it said. *We must be cautious and observe them to be sure that they do not pose a threat to our kind. Remember how our ancestors made that mistake with the Va'alen?*

The answering clicks sounded deflated, as though the pilot had curbed the enthusiasm of the other alien to the point of bringing on a depression.

I know, Father, it said, *but can we not dream that we might be free to explore the galaxy once again? If these visitors can reach us, then surely we can reach beyond our own star once again?*

The pilot's concentration wavered before his son had finished speaking. A blinking, dull orange light flashed slowly lower down on the holo-display to signify an incoming transmission. They didn't send or receive many signals for fear of bringing the Va'alen warships down on their location. That would risk the enemy bombarding the surface or seeking out their ships to destroy them. That had been the bargain; they had to stay on their home world and live in peace or else suffer their wrath if they ventured into space. They were trapped like animals by a superior race of aliens—superior, at least, in strength and war-like tendencies.

What had grabbed the attention of the pilot, making him swipe away the glowing image of the *Ichi*, was the source of the transmission. It came directly from the alien ship that had arrived in their sector and began pumping out tiny devices before turning around and disappearing from and then reappearing on the ship's sensors.

The two creatures on the bridge discussed that in excited, rattling clicks and croaks—these unknown newcomers possessed technology similar to their own. This was technology that the Va'alen had stolen from them generations before and used to conquer the entire system.

He had used the drones that surrounded their planet and ranged ahead of their small, dull red sun to fly directly at the ship to test their responses. The Va'alen would simply open fire on anything threatening the path of one of their warships, but the mysterious newcomers slowed to avoid a collision and instead sent a message out on multiple frequencies.

We are the crew of the Boken Sha. We are from Earth, a planet in the nearest solar system. We mean no harm, we come in peace.

The repeating words meant nothing to them, and the ship's computer tried to decipher the bizarre noises. With the voices came data files—images of a different planet, an alien solar system with just one bright star, structures on the surface of an ash-gray moon and glowing blue domes on a red planet. Images of people who looked slightly like them. Aliens with shorter arms and legs, thicker bodies and tiny heads which couldn't possibly hold a large enough brain to communicate with one another. They had strange skin of different colors, were covered in hair a little like the Va'alen were beneath their armor. All of these images flashed before the large, dark, elliptical eyes as the small mouth opened in an O. This was proof of more intelligent alien life from beyond their system.

The mouth closed as the obvious realization hit hard.

If we received the signal, so will the Va'alen.

The thin fingers swiped away the scrolling pictures. Another gesture brought up the globe-like controls, which were manipulated to spin the smooth, pebble-like craft around and accelerate hard through the darkness. They were headed toward the small exoplanet orbiting the smoldering red dwarf.

—

"Contact, port bow!" The tactical officer yelled a little too loudly, startling a daydreaming Brandt who was taking only her second watch in the big chair. "Moving fast away from us!"

"Shields to maximum, lay in a pursuit course and follow them," Brandt snapped as she hit the ship-wide transmit button. "General quarters, captain to the bridge." She released the button to cut the transmission and barked at the bridge officers as she rose from the chair.

"Are we matching speed and course? Comm—anything?"

"Aye aye," answered the helmswoman.

"Nothing, Commander," the comm officer said.

"Detecting an energy trail, ma'am, similar to our own—"

"What is it?" she asked, just as the bridge door swished open and Torres strode in doing up his flight suit's zipper that he had just shrugged himself into.

"Report," he called out as he walked to take the now-vacated captain's chair.

"Contact. Fast moving with an energy signature similar to our own. Matching course and speed," Brandt said in summary.

"On screen," Torres ordered. "Anything on the comm?"

"Nothing, sir, shall we hail them?"

"Do it," he said. He turned to the tactical officer and asked another question as the comm officer began a loud and professional hail of the unknown craft. "What's the similarity to our energy signature?"

"The echo their engine is leaving is almost the same as ours," he said.

"Cycles are a little slower by the look of it but there's no radiation or other trace. If I had to guess, sir, they're powered by a singularity drive like ours."

"No response to hail, Captain," the comm officer said. Torres acknowledged him efficiently as he turned to the helm. "Can we catch up to them?"

"Not unless we jump, sir," she said, "and we're way too close to the gravity wells of Proxima and the exoplanet to risk that."

Torres stood and thought for a moment.

"Plot their trajectory," he said, knowing the answer as soon as the words left his mouth.

"Proxima Centauri b, sir," the tactical officer said.

"Break off pursuit," Torres said confidently. "Bring us to half current speed and maintain heading. Keep whoever that is on active sensors and monitor all frequencies and continue broadcasting our welcome message."

A chorus of aye, ayes answered his rapid-fire string of orders as he returned to his chair and sat calmly. He waited quietly, hearing the progress reports on their location, their quarry and the lack of response to their hails.

"Approaching the exoplanet, Captain," the helmswoman announced.

"Take us into orbit, keep sca—"

"Captain! Signal detected, it's coming from the surface," the comm officer interrupted him excitedly.

"On screen," he said.

"Audio only, sir."

"On… speaker then," Torres said, sounding deflated that he wouldn't lay eyes on an alien. He had seen extra-terrestrials many times on the old movies he had enjoyed as a kid—he wanted a similar experience now.

The entire bridge crew held their breath as the crackle of the speakers echoed before a rolling, rattling clicking noise sounded. It rose and fell in tempo, with a linguistic cadence.

They could tell it was a deliberate language but not one that they could understand in any way. The crackling sound returned to allow a short period of silence before the noise started again. Nobody spoke as the message played three times, until all of them could recognize the repetition of certain parts. Torres broke the deadlock with a quietly asked question.

"Tactical? I need a full sensor sweep of that planet, and get me coordinates for a point origin on that signal?"

Far below them, on the surface of the tidally locked exoplanet orbiting the small, glowing red star, the smooth-edged craft settled in to land with a whining shriek of thruster engines winding down. Angular landing struts descended and sank into the soft, moist earth. A ramp lowered, and the thin legs of the large-headed creature carried it down quickly before the pebble-like craft shimmered into hazy obscurity to make it almost invisible.

The creature walked towards a knoll of raised ground covered in the black-leafed foliage that carpeted the habitable parts of the planet. After a few steps, it disappeared inside as though it had simply vanished.

It hadn't, but the scattered remnants of their race had learned to hide in plain sight, to use the flowing concealment of nature to shroud their presence against the warmongers who rode roughshod over their entire system.

The creature ignored the shrill croaks of a dozen others like it, having neither the time nor the inclination to explain itself. It went straight to the round chamber and shrugged off the armor that had been so painstakingly attached to it. Doing so left a trail of the pieces that lead to the high-backed chair it had been sitting in when the alien craft had first appeared near their small planet.

It sat, waved long, slender fingers over the rounded plinth to make the display spring to life and tapped confidently at a blinking icon that counted upwards in hieroglyphs. The creature spoke, recording its message and playing it back. When it finished, fingers danced through the air and the shrunken icon that held the recorded message flew off the display and disappeared off the small globe.

Within seconds, the door to the chamber was hammered on repeatedly from the outside. The creature stood to smooth down the crumpled robes that had been disheveled by its armor. The door to the chamber slid open and a shorter creature walked in wearing a look of such fury that the others who followed it shrank away in fear, as though they could *feel* the malevolence radiating from it.

Lighter, higher-pitched croaks and clicks came from it, which went ignored by the creature who had returned in the ship. The shorter intruder walked to the plinth and activated the display, small fingers moving rapidly over the controls until the sent message file was brought up.

The face of the smaller creature stayed neutral but wary as the recorded clip was replayed.

Visitors to this system, it said in their language, *we are the Kuldar. We occupy the first planet near the red sun and we need your help. We beg you, help us.*

The smaller creature turned to the taller one, who sat back down and gave his accuser a blank look. Their facial expressions changed as they each stared into the large, dark eyes of the other. Their feelings and emotions transmitted telepathically between them. Eventually, with an explosive wave of frustration that affected every one of their kind within fifty paces, the shorter one rose quickly and swept from the room.

It turned at the door and shot back a final retort before leaving the chamber.

If they come, husband, you are to be the one to meet them. And if they are a danger to us, you must deal with them yourself. Or else I shall. And if that message brings the Va'alen down on us, there will be a reckoning for you.

With that, the queen left the chamber and her brooding king behind.

CHAPTER 5

Proxima B Orbit

"Captain," flight officer Sarvanto said. He addressed Torres but included in his greeting Brandt and a scientist neither of them had seen before. "We were due to survey this exoplanet in approximately nine days if the thorough plan was to be followed, however this is what we know so far. It's a little smaller than Earth and much closer to the red dwarf it orbits, but the probes show liquid water at the surface, an obvious atmosphere and plant life, just not as we would recognize it."

"How so?" Brandt asked.

This prompted Sarvanto to gesture to the scientist. He stood. A thin man with abnormally large and masculine hands for his small frame, he introduced himself as Cahill. He was an astrophysicist and had evidently been either drafted or volunteered to give the explanation of the unique way that life had evolved on the planet.

"Imagine if you can," he explained in a British accent while moving his hands constantly, "that this planet has permanent night *and* day. It's locked in its orbit. It doesn't rotate like our Earth does around our sun, but then again this sun isn't like ours. It's all low spectrum, red light—"

"*And?*" Torres asked, trying not to sound as impatient as he felt.

"And it may not seem bright, but it's still bombarding the planet with strong UV radiation, so the planet is scorched in one spot."

"Mister Cahill?" Brandt asked as politely as she could. "Any chance you could give us the quick version that doesn't require a lot of prior knowledge on the subject?"

Cahill looked at her with a mixture of dismay and pity, but he did as he was asked. He continued, speaking faster and with less theatrical excitement.

"One side faces the sun all the time and that side is burned in the middle for most of the hemisphere. The other side is in permanent darkness and is about minus fifty degrees for most of it. The only place life can exist, or at least safely exist, is in that ring around the face of the planet where the hot side meets the cold side and creates a kind of... *temperate zone* where the conditions allow for liquid water and for life to exist. There we can see vegetation, but I can't see it being anything like what we would recognize."

"Why?" Torres asked, pleased with the faster explanation.

"Because of the light spectrum," Cahill said. "It's all low spectrum red light and not the white light we have evolved with. You see, the sun is responsible for every living thing on Earth either directly or indirectly. The algae, the grass, the trees; all of these things are the first-level food source for our food's food's food, if you follow? Everything on Earth has evolved for our own spectrum of light. Everything down there has done the same thing with the red light."

"So, no blue skies and green grass?" Brandt asked, clarifying.

"No, ma'am," Cahill answered. "More like permanent emergency lighting and, if I had to guess, black foliage."

"Black?" Torres asked. He frowned and shook his head, dismissing his question as irrelevant. "Is the atmosphere there breathable for us?"

"It *could* be," Cahill said carefully. "But I couldn't say for sure from orbit. It's just a theory as none of the probes have penetrated the atmosphere. From what we can see there are definitely places that look like surface water." Cahill paused before going on, as though there was a strong caveat to his guesswork. "Nitrogen, oxygen, carbon dioxide, helium, methane, hydrogen... it all depends on how they are concentrated at the surface, which I have to be clear—"

"Yeah," Brandt said. "You can't say from orbit."

"Precisely."

"Can we send a probe into the atmosphere?" Torres asked.

"We are, err, working on one, but sadly, we lack the delivery means. If we could requisition a few of your warheads for repurposing, then we might..."

"You can have one. Mister Sarvanto?" Torres addressed the flight officer.

"We have a position for the signal's origin?"

"We do, Captain. Alas nothing visible on sensors."

Torres thanked the two men, watching them take their leave and he was left alone beside Brandt.

She shifted in her seat beside Torres and asked a dozen questions with a single eyebrow twitch. He answered her just as simply.

"Commander, would you kindly lead a team down there for me?"

"Thought you'd never ask."

She rose, trying to keep her excitement locked inside as she dropped a reassuring clenched fist onto her captain's shoulder.

"I'll need Rogers, if you can spare him from the bridge?" she asked.

"He's probably expecting the order," Torres answered.

Brandt left the room and entered the bridge, seeing Rogers's raised eyebrows and boyish smile almost pleading for the chance to join the mission from the helm.

"Fall in, Rogers," she said casually, before leaving the bridge to go see a man about a ghost.

˞

Torres sat alone for a time, swiping his finger slowly up and down the datapad that contained the intelligence about the signal and the planet. He tapped the icon to listen to the rattling, croaking clicks that formed the alien language. The ship's mainframe was still devoting almost a quarter of its processing power to trying to decipher the millions of possible translations.

He flicked over the atmospheric report for the planet, looking at the bizarre graphic that showed a planet with a curious halo of habitable land encircling a scorched circular section. Spinning the image around with his fingers, he zoomed in on the dark hemisphere where the edges were touched by the perma-glacier that covered it. He focused on the strip where the low light of the sun warmed the ground enough that ice gave way to rolling vegetation, wondering if it really was black and not green. That was just one of many unbelievable things he had been faced with in the last few weeks.

With a sigh of resignation, Torres tapped the screen to enlarge the communication subsystem. Inputting his personal authorization code to realign the subspace array, he waited for the call to connect.

And waited.

Eventually the screen sprang to life with the soft tone he had grown accustomed to. Instead of anyone he recognized, a red-eyed face filled the viewscreen wearing a look of fear tinged with excitement. The stranger realized his mistake in failing to gauge the distance to the camera, so he leaned back to reveal a relatively new uniform and an unblemished lieutenant's rank badge on his upper-right chest.

"Hello, sir," the young officer stammered. "Captain Torres."

"No, you're not," Torres said with a smile. "I am."

The boy didn't get the joke and his child-like features melted into uncertainty. He worried he had offended the man that he so idolized. He visibly panicked, stuttering over his words until Torres calmed him down.

"Relax, Lieutenant," he said. He noticed for the first time that the lights of the room behind the young man were dimmed. There seemed to be fewer people than he expected going about their tasks in the control room back on Earth. "Where is everyone?" he asked.

The young officer looked surprised as his eyebrows all but met in the middle. "Sir?"

"It looks abandoned there," Torres said. "And dark."

"Sir, it's almost four in the morning here…" Torres checked the device on his arm as though checking the time would magically change it. The excitement of the unidentified contact and the ensuing hours of busy activity had robbed him of all sense of time. And now that excitement had resulted in his oh-dark-thirty call home.

"So it is, Lieutenant," Torres said recovering himself. "Who is your senior officer tonight?"

"It's err…" the lieutenant hesitated. "It's me, sir."

Torres stopped the next words about to leap from his lips. The kid didn't need to be reminded he seemed young and inexperienced.

"Lieutenant, can I suggest you go and find someone with a clearance much higher than your own? Tell them it's a code nineteen." The look of incomprehension on the young face looking back at him made Torres realize that the junior officer left in charge wasn't fully briefed about their mission.

"Yes, sir," he responded. "Code one-niner. Call back in ten mikes?"

"Affirmative," Torres said, hitting the icon to terminate the call. Ten minutes spent in silent contemplation later, Torres placed the call again. This time it was answered after only seconds. The screen popped up huge and he saw three faces crammed into the view. Behind them, almost jumping up to see was what he guessed to be the young lieutenant. One of the three faces vying for primacy in front of the screen noticed the young man, turned and glared until he got the message and left the room.

They were all in PT kit: sweatpants and hoodies used as comfortable, off-duty clothing. All three appear to have been roused in a hurry.

"Captain Torres," the stern woman with the short haircut in the center announced. "You're on with Crawford from UNID, Admiral Tozer—" the gray-haired man to her left raised a hand in greeting "—and Mister Chen from Hyper."

"Good morning everyone," Torres said. "I apologize for the hour, but I am about to order a mission to the surface of an exoplanet that we believe is inhabited."

The two men started talking at once, each drowning out the other's question with his own. Both Torres and Crawford shrank slightly from the sensory overload.

"One at a time, please, gentlemen," she said.

"Are they capable of faster-than-light travel?" the admiral asked.

"Are there any signs of hostility?" the Chinese guy from Hyper asked.

"Both unknown at this time. You'll be updated after the mission, but in the meantime," Torres tapped at the datapad, "here is everything we have on the current situation. If there are no more questions?"

"Just one," Crawford said. "What is a code nineteen? I can't see any reference to it in the mission briefing."

"A code nineteen is a means to get an excited young officer to wake up the people who know what's going on." He smiled slightly. "Torres out."

~

"Specter," Brandt said, greeting the man she still thought of as an old friend. She still wasn't used to holding him at a distance like a work colleague and not engaging on the more intimate level they shared previously. "You up for a trip to shore?"

"Happily, Commander," he said. Specter rose and began to disconnect his suit—his *body*—from the diagnostic wires running from his abdomen to the terminal in the lab. "I have reviewed the data on the exoplanet, and I presume you'll want a small recon team in full armor?"

"Yeah," Brandt answered simply.

"What configuration do you need from me?" he asked. "Configuration?"

"I am able to adapt my loadout for fire support, sniper, recon, close quarter conflict, stealth and urban covert…"

"CQ, please," she said. The environment on the surface of the planet was dark, and this minimized the chance of engaging any enemy at distance. "Docking bay in ten?"

"Of course, Commander," he said, his scarred face giving her a small smile that threw her memories into a spiral. The face and the voice of her old friend radiated at her behind the terse and formal words of this… *robot* they'd rebuilt in a lab somewhere.

Brandt walked to the armory, then stepped into her suit and wriggled her left arm as a knot of material from her flight suit caught uncomfortably. This obstruction forced her to open the suit and adjust it before sealing herself up once again. She took a pistol and a carbine, loading herself out with full complement of charged magazines and fitting the singularity pods to the weapons. She sighed to herself, in apprehension about the drop that would take her directly to the docking bay below. Her helmet blinked into life as the HUD came online. She stepped inside the tube, weapons locked to her metal skin, and crossed her arms across her body. The plate beneath her feet slid away quickly and dropped her down.

She clanged to the deck of the docking bay. Her left knee bent to absorb the energy as she placed her left palm out to stop her downward momentum and threw her right hand out to her side to balance her upper body.

"Awesome!" Rogers yelled as he ducked under the stubby delta wing of the *Tanto* to pop upright wearing a massive grin. "You did a superhero landing!"

"I did a what?" Brandt asked as she stood, annoyed with herself. She should have been able to catch the movement in time and not drop to her knee.

"You did the thing… with the knee and the hand…? Aaahh, forget it," Rogers said, recovering his professionalism just in time for everyone to ignore his comments.

Brandt dismissed his words with a shake of her head and called out to her team.

"Okay, when we get to the surface I want Specter on point, with me and Eze behind and Butler at the tail. Marcus, Byrne and

Chopra: stay and guard the LZ under the command of Zero. I don't want anything eating Rogers."

Those suited soldiers she named, the current team on standby, gave away their acknowledgments through shifts in body language. The one team member not named also shifted, looking around and checking if anyone else had been omitted from a task. Brandt addressed his growing disappointment.

"Davis, I want you on one of the gun turrets," she said, "and organize three others from the off-duty roster to suit up with you. Watch our backs up here, okay?"

"Yes, ma'am," he rumbled, clearly unhappy at not getting to go down to the surface.

"You'll get your chance," Brandt told him. He perked up a little and nodded. She turned, walked along the line of suited soldiers to inspect their armor and loadout. Her HUD flashed red on their outlines, giving her their basic information. She blinked to add them to her current team selection—far quicker and more intrinsic than having to use the wrist-mounted device with the last generation of technology.

She assigned them to alpha and bravo teams, the former with her and the latter guarding their ship and pilot, and then paused as she got to Specter. She'd managed to stop thinking of him as Jake and watched as his readout gave her no information other than his callsign. She scrolled through the options with his suit, which differed slightly from theirs in many ways, and she opened a private comm channel between them.

"I need your vitals on my HUD," she instructed.

"Commander, my vitals aren't exactly standard," he explained. "My heart rate and blood pressure would register as dangerously low for you because—"

"Understood," she said, not wanting to re-live the details of his arms and legs being blown away. She didn't need to learn about whatever else they did to him in a lab over the years she had thought him dead. "Can you give me anything to monitor?"

A pause hung before he answered. "Giving you basic brainwave activity, Commander. That should satisfy your needs?"

It did. Brandt cut the link before their silence became noticeable to the rest of the team. She called out for them to board and stepped on the tail ramp of the *Tanto* ready to be the first person to set foot on an alien world.

CHAPTER 6

Deep Space Between Earth and Mars

"All ship systems report ready for jump, Admiral," one of the tactical officers on the bridge of the *Venture* called out.

There were almost three times as many bridge officers than there were on the distant *Ichi*. *Venture* was a far larger ship and acted as the focal point for the three other big deep space vessels in the fleet family. It also had to manage the dozens of smaller dropships flying between them all,

"Order the rest of the fleet to close all docking bays and hold current positions. I want us at least a thousand kilometers away when we jump. Sound general quarters."

"Aye, aye, sir," one of the comm officers—the one responsible for inter-fleet traffic—answered.

He called into the mic on his wireless headset. A single klaxon, muted so as not to cause panic onboard, sounded long and insistently to give the entire crew the order to lock down. It was the same signal they used when approaching danger. It communicated to the crew not quite battle stations but almost, and Admiral Dassiova reckoned that an inaugural faster-than-light jump qualified.

He surreptitiously wiped the palms of both hands in turn on the pant legs of his flight suit. He now bore the admiral's crest on the right side of his suit and his name on the left, just above the embroidered legend of *Venture*. He resisted the urge to stroke the name of his ship, to feel the bumps of the stitching beneath his fingertips to reassure him in his hidden superstitions.

Dassiova waited.

He waited until the helmsman called out their all-stop after forging ahead the required distance to leave the rest of the fleet behind.

"Comm? Get me Captain Wright," he said.

The officer turned away and tapped at his display, turning again to nod at the admiral in his chair not unlike a throne. Dassiova stood, announcing that he'd take the call in his quarters before stepping to the suite of staterooms off the main bridge. He tapped the screen of the data terminal at his desk and saw the connected call waiting to go through. He liked it when his troops recognized what he wanted and did it, as the comm officer did putting the call through to the right terminal without needing to be instructed.

"Captain," Dassiova said stiffly when the red face of the *UNS Cortez*'s commanding officer came on screen.

This man had wanted his job, had wanted command of the entire fleet after missing out of the captaincy of the recon mission, but he had bowed to Dassiova's appointment with some grace. The two had agreed to accept each other's position without malice or agenda. In truth, Wright recognized that they needed a warrior's mentality in overall command, but he hoped that Dassiova in turn recognized his experience and natural ability to command multiple ships in deep space.

"Admiral," he responded in an equable tone. He seemed to also be in his private quarters, judging by the surroundings Dassiova could see behind the man's head. "Are you ready to proceed with the jump?"

"We are," he said. "Captain, you have command of the fleet until such time as we are reunited. I will send orders via subspace relay when we arrive at our jump point for our escort ships to follow."

"Understood," Wright answered with a solemn pride. "Safe journey."

Dassiova killed the call, rising from his desk and returning to the bridge.

The relief flight officer stood from the command chair without ceremony. There was no announcement of Dassiova's presence. He had put a stop to all of that. He didn't need his ego massaged; it got in the way of efficiency as far as he was concerned. He preferred his crew to be watching their allocated stations rather than kissing his ass. He took his seat, confirmed that general quarters had been reported complete, and checked again with the engineering team working on the Fold Drive.

"Confirm we have a green light on all adjustments?" he said into the comm.

He received an emphatic affirmative from the other end. The admiral nodded to himself.

Now or never.

Protocol dictated that he should have ordered one of the frigates to jump first and test the last calibrations, but since every ship had to be individually tweaked the risks were equal to all of them. He would be endangering the lives of all six thousand men and women on the *Venture* regardless of whether he let someone else go first. He was not the kind of man to let someone else take a risk just because he was higher up the food chain.

"Helm: our course is plotted?" he barked with an edge of excited anticipation touching his words.

"Yes, sir."

"Stand by for thirty-second activation of the drive on my mark," Dassiova said, managing to hide the stress in his voice. He paused. "*Initiate.*"

From the bridge of the *Cortez* on the viewscreen at high magnification, the larger profile of the *Venture* seemed to wobble. The lines of it became obscured by extreme vibration. With a small and almost anti-climactic dull pop of light it disappeared. The ship simply wasn't there any longer.

Captain Wright stood and watched the admiral's ship vanish. He counted off the thirty seconds silently behind his neutral expression and covered his worry when he reached thirty-nine and still nobody had spoken. Just as he took in a breath to release the tension growing inside him, the comm officer nearly jumped clean out of their chair.

"Captain, subspace communication incoming. It's the *Venture*, sir."

Wright relaxed in relief and called for the transmission to be put on-screen. Dassiova's face replaced the blank wall ahead of them and even the stone-cold admiral couldn't hide his smile.

"Captain Wright," he said, "transmitting our current co-ordinates to you now..."

Wright looked down at a display, watching the numbers be translated onto a three-dimensional star chart of their solar system. His eyes went wide. The *Venture* had halved the distance between themselves and Mars in under a minute. Dassiova spoke again, his voice serious as he gave the orders that would break them away from their pre-set course.

"Captain, plot course for rendezvous point Echo. Signal the *Hammer* and the *Norton* to jump in turn and we'll meet you there. Send the agreed signal to Earth when you go. *Venture* out."

Captain Wright relayed the orders to his comm officers, sending first the *Norton* and then the *Hammer* to their agreed meeting place. Both ships soon reported back that they had arrived safely and that they had sensors detecting the *Venture* arriving roughly eight thousand kilometers away from them. Wright turned and ordered his comm officer to record a message. The bridge went quiet and Wright cleared his throat.

"Earth Control, this is Captain Wright of the *UNS Cortez* with the Ninth Fleet. We are at..." he paused, looking down for their precise co-ordinates before relaying them, "...and we are experiencing a number of engine and electrical failures. Be advised our estimated time of arrival to Mars is currently plus-twenty-one days unless we can affect repairs in transit. No requirement for assistance to be sent from either Earth or Mars at this time. *Cortez* out."

He nodded, and the recording was cut. By the time that message arrived at Earth, they would have to wait over a month for any signal to reach their home planet from the Mars base regarding the fleet's overdue arrival. That gave the fleet a little over four weeks to get to Proxima and back to Mars before anyone in their own system would ever know that they hadn't been limping along on their slow Red Run.

Wright smiled, trying not to show excitement. He felt too much emotion was unbecoming of a captain, but he could barely contain himself.

"Plot a course," he said.

"Ready for your order, sir," his flight officer said. Wright took his seat, leaning to one side as a smirk tickled one corner of his mouth. "Initiate jump."

The Fold Drive of the *Cortez* activated, bending time and space through the manipulation of electromagnetic waves to shorten the distance between two distantly separated parts of the galaxy. Wright sensed a jolt, a fraction of a second when he felt as though he was falling, and a wave of nausea until he steadied himself on the arms of his chair. A hum of noiseless echo filled the bridge. It seemed almost like the absence of noise; there was none of the usual buzz of a large ship existing like a massive, metal organism. They called this passage subspace, as though this was a physical place and not a state of non-existence apart from the universe they had inhabited only moments before. After the pre-determined time spent in that state—what they were calling Fold Space—the power to the drive was cut and they reappeared in normal space.

Immediately, loud klaxons and warning sirens shrieked at them as the tactical officer yelled a collision warning.

"Forty kilometers, dead ahead!" he screamed. "Evasive maneuvers!"

The man at the helm required no confirmation or repetition of those orders. Crashing a ninety-five-thousand-ton spaceship into a one-hundred-forty-thousand-ton spaceship was never a good idea in anyone's world.

The *Cortez* had dropped back into real space directly side-on to the flank of the *Venture*. Luckily their bridge crew was just as alert as the *Cortez*'s, because the two ships engaged engines and maneuvering thrusters fired at full to push and pull their behemoth vessels away from the impending collision. The *Venture* went directly upward in their own evasion as the *Cortez* slammed everything she had into reverse and pointed her nose down to dive below them.

"Cut shields," Wright barked as he looked directly at the tactical officer, who simply stared back in horror as his fingers fluttered uncertainly at the controls. "Do it now!"

He had no time to explain. A collision of that epic proportion, even with the forward shields at maximum, would crush both ships and cause huge, probably fatal damage. Their unexposed hulls would do the same amount of catastrophic damage to one another. But the sudden absence of a shield removed a near quarter of a kilometer that the shield array extended away from their hull, and allowed for a greater distance from their target.

Unluckily for them, nobody onboard the *Venture* had that thought in time. The furthest projection of their ship smashed into the shields and buckled, crumpling the long spike of the Fold Drive emitter. The impact sheared off the destroyed array, which usually protruded ahead of their shields to allow them to fold the space ahead of them. Everyone onboard the *Cortez* held their breath as the collision warning sirens blared ship-wide. The helmsman could do no more; he had turned their big vessel into a steep nosedive and activated every engine and thruster they had to push them away from their big sister.

Agonizing seconds ticked by until the sirens stopped shrieking as suddenly as they had started.

"Clear, sir," the tactical officer called out, his voice cracking as he spoke.

Wright looked at the helmsman, seeing the beads of sweat on his bald dome as he looked up nervously.

"Well done, helmsman," Wright said carefully, forcing the shake out of his words. He looked at the man's name on his flight uniform. "Moon?"

"Yes, sir?" helmsman Moon answered.

"Very good job," Wright told him with a reassuring hand on his shoulder as he walked back towards his chair. "Damage report?"

"Sir, engineering reports that the Fold Drive emitter is offline. No way of knowing how bad until they do an EVA and check it out."

"Sir, Admiral Dassiova on comm," one of the other bridge crew-members said to Wright.

"I'll take it in my quarters," Wright said. He walked stiffly toward the door that hissed open to admit him to the captain's staterooms. As soon as the door hissed shut behind him, his knees went weak and threatened to pitch him to the deck. He let out the breath he had been holding and panted hard for a few seconds as his chest heaved and he fought down the urge to vomit. He stood, getting a hold of himself. He unashamedly took a long pour from a bottle of Japanese whiskey before drinking it down in two gulps.

The liquor steadied him; he had never had a problem with it, but at times like this it was good to celebrate still being alive. He restored the glass to its place beside the bottle and sat at his desk. The screen blinked to life at his touch to reveal an ashen-faced admiral.

"What the *hell* just happened, Wright?" Dassiova said anxiously.

"That," Wright said wistfully, "was a *bloody* close call."

"You're telling me. We need to change protocols because we can't be jumping into one another like that; it's too damned risky. Any damage?"

"Our Fold Drive emitter took the hit against your shields," he said, unwittingly allowing a hint of accusation taint his words. He spoke quickly, shifting his tone. "I'm sure it can be fixed up soon enough."

Dassiova swore and chewed at his lip, no doubt deciding whether to leave them behind until they could affect repairs.

"Okay, report to me when you have an estimate, and, Captain?" Wright looked directly at him. "Thanks. Your crew did well not to hit us."

"As did yours, Admiral," Wright said. He left out the fact that if anyone on the admiral's bridge had thought to drop their shields, then they wouldn't be faced with the situation they currently in. "*Cortez* out."

The damage was, on the balance of what *could've* been, pretty minor. The *Cortez* had lost the forward eight meters of their Fold Drive spike that housed the emitter, but they had over a dozen replacement parts among the rest of the fleet.

Engineering reported an eighteen-hour minimum turnaround to refit the part. In response, the captain gave them ten hours and a reassurance that he knew they were the best engineers in the entire UN and would get it done. He reported the time delay to the admiral who, understandably, was unhappy at losing any time.

"Sir, if I may?" Wright asked. Dassiova nodded his assent for the man to speak freely.

"We're only three jumps at maximum safe distance away from the objective from this location; perhaps you could send a frigate and follow them, if we were to be afforded the remaining escort and meet you there?"

Dassiova seemed to mull the suggestion over, promising to take the idea into consideration and get back to him. "Don't waste any time, Captain; get those repairs underway immediately."

"Already in hand, sir."

Dassiova, with his senior flight officer beside him, placed the call through the subspace array in his cabins. The call went through straightaway and showed a buzz of activity going on behind the uniformed officer who answered.

"Admiral," she said in greeting.

Dassiova didn't know the woman but addressed her by the insignia on her shoulder.

"Commander, I have a sitrep which is a cause for some concern, if the senior officers are available?"

"Sorry, Admiral," she said back in clipped, professional tones. "Currently they are engaged on an urgent matter and I'm waiting on authorization to bring you into that particular loop. Go with your sitrep, sir."

Dassiova ignored all of the information she gave that he couldn't affect, registering it and filing it all away for later. He proceeded to give his report.

"We have successfully jumped the fleet beyond the Oort cloud," he said, "and our last transmission to Earth gives us a little over forty-one days until our absence from the system will prompt questions from other territories. We did, however, experience an issue when the *Cortez* jumped into the RV and we narrowly avoided a collision with them. That caused damage to the Fold Drive emitter of the *Cortez*, which will take eighteen hours to repair. The *Hammer*, the *Norton* and the *Venture* are undamaged." He paused before offering the solution to the problems he had just laid on the messenger. "I propose that we jump the *Hammer* ahead to be followed by the *Venture*, leaving the *Norton* behind to protect the *Cortez* until she can join us."

"All noted, Admiral," the commander said in a flat tone. "Re-establish communications in one hour. Earth out."

The screen went black before Dassiova could respond, prompting a surge of anger to rise up inside him. He took a breath and allowed it to dissipate before he did or said something immature and not becoming of a fleet admiral.

"Cold-ass bitch," he muttered, gaining a stifled snigger from his flight officer, Suranne Massey. He turned to her, making the laugh dissolve instantly. Instead of remonstrating with her, he asked her opinion on what they should do.

"Well, sir," Massey said, "unless Earth has any more intel that makes the urgency of getting to Proxima a priority, my thoughts would be to keep the fleet as one. It's not exactly bad out here, is it?" She smiled, unveiling herself as a human being with a playful side instead of the cold, calculating executive officer he needed to keep a ship of that size running smoothly. It was a small city, by all accounts, much like the ancient floating cities that housed the old earth planes from generations ago. Back then they floated on the water and were powered by nuclear reactors, which had long been jettisoned off into deep space.

He looked out of the wide viewport in his office, which formed the first of the plush cabins that comprised his private quarters. This first room was for senior officer meetings and communications, but further inside were the cabins where none of the crew bar the service personnel had been.

"Yeah," Dassiova said as he stared out at the empty blackness of space. "Almost every shiny dot you see out there is already dead. Gone. Extinguished long before you or I were even born. It's.... it's *humbling.*"

"It is that, sir," his flight officer answered. "But it's also pretty goddamned cool. Think about it; we're the first humans to go beyond our solar system, apart from the recon ship, so we're the first ones to actually see these stars before they burn out to nothing. Think of the possibilities." She stepped nearer his shoulder and leaned in so close that he could smell her hair. "You see that one?" she asked him, leaning over more and pointing a slender arm past his face so that he could follow the line of her forearm extending to her index finger.

He caught a wave of her scent and tried to ignore how it made him feel.

"Yes…"

"That's where we're going," she said wistfully, "past the dull red one to see if we can find a place that life exists. So we can mine precious minerals and bring back the resources to Earth and maybe one day create another place there where we can live. Perhaps our grandchildren will be born there? Or else their children? Maybe we will have statues erected for us, on the new world or the old one, for the intrepid discoverers that found another planet for humanity to expand and conquer the galaxy."

Dassiova's face dropped.

"Perhaps those planets are already occupied. Perhaps we will jump into a new system and spark a war that ends humanity. Perhaps we invite a war on Earth that ruins civilizations hundreds—*thousands*—of years old and we just threw all that away because we had an engine that could take us somewhere we weren't supposed to be."

"You think that's right?" Massey snapped, pulling away from him slightly. "You think humanity was supposed to be confined to one single planet? You think we should have stayed as stupid monkeys eating bananas and not invented tools, or the wheel, or steam power?

You think there should have been no industrial revolution? No discovery of fossil fuels and the massive leaps in technology that followed? You think we shouldn't have discovered how to split an atom and use nuclear power when it exists in the universe ready to be so exploited? You think that we shouldn't have discovered the singularity tech and not used it to get to the moon and create domes to live under? Same for Mars—you think we shouldn't be there mining for the rich ores we can't even get on Earth? Sir, forgive me being so forward, but if you believe that, then why the *hell* are you commanding this mission?"

Dassiova turned and regarded the passionate woman just as coldly as he had been addressed from Earth.

"You think that just because I worry that we shouldn't be pushing so far beyond our natural capabilities that I believe less in this mission than you do?" he asked in a cold voice that chilled her through to the core. "You think that just because I have moral and existential doubts about what we're doing out here, that I am too weak to command?"

She quailed under his quiet onslaught. "No, sir." She took a half step back and put her head down slightly. "It's just that I believe, with all my heart, that we need to push the boundaries of exploration as far as we can to give humanity the best chance of survival. It's our *duty*."

"It may be just that," Dassiova replied, "but my first duty is to the people of this fleet."

CHAPTER 7

Proxima B Surface

"Specter, take point," Brandt said. The tail ramp of the *Tanto* hit the moist surface and sank into the dark, almost purple moss that grew there. After they had landed, the team spread out in all-around defense.

"Roger," Specter said. "Moving, bearing twenty-eight degrees north."

The rest of the four-man team fell in, following the lead of their cybernetic warrior. He set a pace far faster than any of the rest of his wholly human team could match, even in their armor. Their suits had assessed the atmosphere in a few seconds, and found it breathable with a slightly reduced oxygen content than they were used to. Breathing on this planet would be similar to breathing at high altitude on Earth. Brandt reassured herself that it would just be like her experience training at higher altitude. Specter didn't have most of a body to provide the precious oxygen to; instead he had an almost infinite onboard power source that could keep him alive even in an unbreathable atmosphere for a time.

"Jake! Jesus, slow *down*!" Brandt called into the squad comm after half a mile. She cursed herself for calling him by the name he had once gone by.

"Sorry," he said. "I sometimes forget when I'm working with… with *humans*."

"Dude," Brandt countered, "you *are* human, just seriously up-graded. Give the rest of us non-augmented types a chance?"

"I apologize, Commander," he said over the comm. "I'm... I'm just *excited*, I think..."

"It's okay," she told him. "We're all excited, only we can't maintain the pace you're setting. Slow it down."

"Affirmative," Specter said. "Approaching target coordinates in one point seven clicks." "Roger that. Half pace and go carefully."

Specter acknowledged her orders and slowed his pace to one that the mere humans could match. Though slowed, he still pressed on, diligently through the curiously dark foliage that none of them had ever seen before. Far behind them, spread out to guard their invaluable shuttlecraft, were four other members of the team under the command of the sniper she had known a lifetime ago.

"Zero, Grip," she said into the mic.

"Go," he responded.

"Status report?"

"All good in the hood," he said. The skin around Brandt's eyes tightened as she sucked in a sharp breath through her nose. Zero knew non-standard comm language always annoyed her, and he knew that she knew he did it deliberately.

"Push out to one-fifty; keep our bird safe," she said.

"Affirmative," he replied in a cold, low tone that meant business. "Moving."

They pushed onward, Specter dictating the distance and bearing to target from his own HUD. He moved in silence, a feat made easier by the plush and moist moss that covered the ground, though it occasionally made for treacherous footing. A hidden dip in the bizarre landscape was too easily obscured by the groundcover.

The team had landed only a few kilometers away from the signal's point of origin, but the way that this dark, muted planet supported and nurtured life was fascinating, distracting and slowed their short walk. A band of habitable ground only twenty miles wide was hedged by scorched deserts on the inside and frozen glaciers on the other, and they found themselves having to avoid what looked like a well-worn path running along the center of that livable land.

As he moved, Specter found himself experiencing things he had not felt for years. Feelings that he didn't associate with Specter, but that had belonged to Jake Santana before him. He felt excitement, he knew that, but he also felt a nervous trepidation about their approach. As he was trying to understand this, his enhanced eyes detected something through the visor. He froze and gave the hand signal for the others to do the same before he sent them scampering for cover. The HUD could detect nothing in the low light, but his eyes did, even if he couldn't be sure what he was detecting.

Then he saw it. Long, slender limbs and a large head. Dark, almost black elliptical eyes shining with the smallest of reflections until the almost imperceptible flash of tiny movement gave them away.

A blink; gone almost immediately, but something had definitely been there.

"Specter," Brandt called softly to him. "What's the deal?"

"There's something here, Commander," he said. "It isn't registering on the HUD, but there is something nearby. Something alive."

"How do you know?" Eze asked.

"Because I think I'm looking at it ... and I think it's looking straight at me."

With those words, the thing he couldn't quite make out blinked again, confirming its existence. The others behind tried to adjust the optical feeds on their suits to improve their vision. Specter didn't need to do that; he could now make the creature out clearly as it shifted position. It seemed to stare right at him —right *through* him—and he felt a sense of hope and relief wash over him. He knew, or he was fairly certain, that these feelings came from the alien and not himself. Those feelings changed to fear in a heartbeat when Brandt readied her weapon instinctively as soon as she saw it.

Ignoring what was being said behind him, Specter lowered his own gun and stepped out to approach slowly with his hands held open. "It's alright," he said aloud.

"Specter," Brandt hissed, "stand down!"

"It's okay, Commander," he told her. "It doesn't want to hurt us."

"He's right," Eze said curiously. "It needs our help."

Allowing herself to take in the scene, Brandt suddenly felt it too: the wave of emotion lapping at her consciousness.

The creature, tall and renowned among the remnant of its people, wore no armor and carried no weapons. It stood to its full height, taller than the aliens approaching, and stepped away from the cover of the tree it had been partly hiding behind. Facing the one walking toward it, the creature bent down slightly to meet the visor at what it guessed was eye-level. Making a long and formal introduction, it radiated a sense of welcome and genuine hope that these aliens from another system possessed the technology to save their race. The words made no sense to the visitors, but it hoped that they could sense the feeling and emotion it tried to convey.

For these visitors, these aliens, to have no sense of empathy could be catastrophic for the creature's race but there were no choices left. No options available.

They needed help, or they would perish.

Overwhelmed by the emotions he felt, Specter raised his right hand and held it out toward the alien. He couldn't have said why. He felt that a touch, a physical connection, would solidify their peaceful greeting. Slowly, tentatively, the slender fingers of the alien reached out to touch the tips against his own artificial hand.

"Captain Torres," said the suited UNID member on the screen. "We've analyzed the document you sent and believe we may actually be able to help you. The cra…" She paused, narrowing her eyes at Torres. "Captain, confirm that you are confidential your end? There are no crew members who don't have classified clearance with you?"

"Just me," Torres responded flatly.

"Very well. The craft we recovered on Earth back in the twenty-second century provided a lot of the hieroglyphs you received, and people working on that have had some time to translate them. They started with the easy stuff like figuring out what the switch or component was on the crashed vessel and matching it up with that 'glyph to start making a kind of alphabet." She paused, waiting to see if Torres was still following her.

"Go on," he said, a hint of annoyance in his words.

"Well, their language doesn't use an alphabet like ours. Our best guess is that each 'glyph is a phrase, or a terminology as opposed to using their ABCs."

Torres fought down the urge to facepalm and let out a loud groan of exasperation. All those years of study and the only thing they could say for sure was that they didn't know. It wasn't like the ancient Egyptians had an alphabetized system that English speakers could understand, but they seemed to work that out easily enough without supercomputers. He hoped that the story had a better outcome than where her tone was leading him.

"So, can you decipher it or not?" he snapped, more harshly than he intended.

"Yes, and no," she said unhelpfully. "The best we can do is actually marry it up to old hieroglyphs found on Earth and use that as a reference."

Interesting, he thought.

"We have a beta program able to run those simulations and have deciphered some of what you received. Transmitting that and the program to you now."

Torres glanced at the edge of his data terminal and saw the blinking icon showing an incoming file transfer. He activated it and watched the progress bar fill up rapidly.

"Got it," he said. "Anything else?"

"Negative, Captain."

"Good, Torres out." He killed the link, bringing up the file and looking at the partly translated phrases in between the alien symbols.

Strangers … home. We are termed … primary astral body … bordering red sun … provide aid … plead and supplicate … provide aid.

"Well…" he said with wide eyes, "if *that's* to be believed, Mister Sarvanto, then I think these guys might need our help."

Sarvanto stepped forward from where he had been standing behind the viewscreen on Torres's orders. He didn't hold the same level of clearance as the captain, but that wasn't to say that the captain didn't trust in the opinions of the officers he commanded. The Scandinavian leaned over the desk beside Torres as he took in the partial translation and *hmmm*'d pensively.

"I think you are right, sir," he said. "We should probably let the ground team know as a matter of urgency?"

Torres tapped the screen to open a secure link to Brandt. Since she was in command on the ground, it would be for her to decide how best to inform the rest of her team. Torres hated that part; having to sit in orbit and send people down into potential danger. His instincts told him he should be taking point on those maneuvers himself.

"Brandt, go ahead." Her breathless voice sprang from the speakers.

"It's Torres. Sitrep?"

"We… we've established, or at least I *think* we've established, first contact with a sentient, extra-terrestrial species."

CHAPTER 8

Deep Space Beyond Earth's Solar System

"Admiral, we have Earth on subspace ahead of schedule," the comm officer announced.

Hearing the words, Dassiova rose and walked toward his cabins with a nod of acknowledgment to the officer. Dassiova sat, waiting for the call to be linked to his terminal and worrying about what could have happened for them to be calling back ahead of schedule. It was a risk making the call, as the emitters would doubtless give off a signal that other territories could detect.

"Dassiova here," he said as he hit the icon to connect the subspace call.

"Admiral," the same commander said in a bullish tone, "you are ordered to proceed to Proxima Centauri b with all haste. Take as many of the Ninth Fleet's resources as you are able to bring. You are specifically ordered not to leave an escort frigate behind to guard the *Cortez* and offload as many of their fighting reserves as possible. Further orders will be transmitted when you report in from the Centauri system."

"What's changed?" he asked her.

"Admiral, I'm not at liberty to divulge anything other than that the crew of the *Boken sha Ichi* are reporting first contact with an alien race. Proceed with caution and prepare for battle stations. Earth out."

"Cold bitch," Dassiova said again. He leaned back and tried to comprehend the gravity of the information and the orders he had been given. He could not disobey those orders, but neither was he willing to abandon a stranded crew of around four thousand souls. They were so far from any habitable planet that they would all die of old age or starvation without a working Fold Drive. He decided to leave them with their full complement and called the captain of one of their frigate escorts, the *Norton*, to advise him that the *Norton* required immediate diagnostic work to be logged on their own Fold Drive.

"I'm sure a power surge was recorded during your last jump, wasn't it?" He enquired innocently, glad that the shrewd man grasped the fact quickly.

"Indeed, Admiral," he said with a smirk. "In fact I'm certain I logged the issue with you shortly after you arrived here. At least that's what my comm logs will show, I'm sure."

"Good man," Dassiova said before terminating the call. He told Massey what he wanted, organizing for the *Hammer* to jump ahead of them by only thirty seconds, but for their target co-ordinates to be spread further apart so that there couldn't be a repeat of the near-disaster of their last jump.

"How is it," Massey, his flight officer mused, "that our comm links through subspace are pinpoint accurate, yet our ships can't jump to the precise locations we want them to?"

"Something to do with the size of the hole punched through space-time, apparently," Dassiova told her. "That's what they told me when I asked the exact same question."

"So, the smaller the ship, the more accurate the jump?"

"No idea. Prepare us for jump." She nodded and left, leaving him scratching his chin apprehensively. They were about to make the biggest faster-than-light jump in the history of humanity.

Captain Wright acknowledged his orders, expressing his gratitude for the escort being left behind despite the orders to the contrary.

"Nothing to do with me, Captain," Dassiova said. "The *Norton* has to be thorough and investigate that power surge they experienced. It would be reckless of them to jump without running a diagnostic that should take, oh, say eighteen hours?"

"A touch of fate, Admiral," Wright agreed with a smirk, before signing off and wishing them good luck.

Dassiova sat in his chair and caught the eye of a comm officer. "Inform the captain of the *Hammer* that I'm making an announcement, and then get me a ship-wide channel for us and the *Hammer*."

He gave the admiral an aye, aye and hit the icons on his screen. Once the other ship had been reached, he turned back and nodded. Dassiova hit the transmit button.

"Crews of the *Venture* and the *Hammer*, this is Admiral Dassiova," he began, with and strength and resolve in his tone. "We have been informed that the recon crew of the *Bōken sha Ichi* have made first contact with intelligent alien lifeforms. I'll repeat that, because I think it warrants being repeated. Humanity has made first contact with an alien race. We have been requested to proceed with all haste to support the recon crew, which is what we are doing now. God speed and see you all on the other side. Dassiova out."

"Course plotted, sir," his helmsman called out.

"Signal the *Hammer* to jump," he said. He looked down at the three-dimensional display and watched as the symbol for one of their identical frigates simply vanished from the readout. He took his seat and looked dead ahead.

"Initiate jump."

Proxima B Surface

"Captain," Brandt whispered inside her helmet, "tell me you're seeing this?"

"Affirmative," Torres answered, his eyes glued to the screen in his quarters as he watched the live link to his ground commander's suit system.

He had no words as he watched in awe. The creature, the alien being, crouched beside a round plinth in a dimly lit room that didn't have a single straight edge. It invited the shadowy figure opposite it, Specter, to crouch similarly. The creature waved slender fingers over the plinth to make it erupt into life and show their ship represented with tiny holographic pixels. He tapped at it; his fingers seemed to hit only air but the interface responded and their message replayed through hidden speakers.

We are the crew of the Boken Sha. We are from Earth, a planet in the nearest solar system. We mean no harm, we come in peace.

Torres's voice came back to him via the suit link, and the alien first pointed to the display, then pointed to Specter.

"That's us," he said, pointing at the display of their ship. "We sent it from this, up there…" He pointed upward, through the earthen ceiling and the thousand kilometers of low light into the space above them.

It made rattling noises in its throat, croaking like an Earth amphibian.

"Commander," Torres said, "I'm uploading a translation program to your suits now. It's geared for their hieroglyphic alphabet, but the translation software should be able to start learning."

Brandt acknowledged him. The existence of a translation program was news to her, but not unexpected. Perhaps the beings they were talking to now were of the same race as the ones who had crashlanded on Earth thousands of years ago. That assimilation of facts nagged at her with questions, but the scene before her claimed her attention. With a live subject to work with, their translation software should start to recognize the sounds it made and associate them with words in English.

Her suit registered the upload and she opened the program. She pushed it to the background of her display, as she was still mesmerized watching the alien and the cyborg pointing at things and saying their names.

The alien pointed to itself and made a recognizable sound which it repeated a few times. The suit translation software, running minimized in the lower left quadrant of Brandt's field of vision, came up with two syllables written phonetically.

"Kul-dar."

Specter saw it too. "Kuldar? Your name is Kuldar?"

"Kuldar," the alien hissed uncertainly. It seemed to lack the same kind of vocal chords that the visiting humans possessed. It breathed out, making its mouth and lips frame the same shape that Specter's had made. Specter alone had removed his helmet, as he alone among them could still access the necessary HUD features through his ocular implants.

"Specter," Specter said slowly, carefully pronouncing the two syllables as he pointed to himself.

"*Spec-terr?*" the alien hissed, waving a bony hand to incorporate the other three.

"Humans," Brandt said on impulse.

She hesitated briefly before accessing the release feature on her suit. The sudden action made the alien jump in fright slightly as the suit sprang open in sections to let her step forward unprotected. She held up a hand to try and soothe the alien, but it recovered quickly and reached out to touch its fingertips to hers. She tried not to recoil as the cool, soft, leathery skin touched her own.

"We are humans," she said slowly and softly, "from Earth."

The alien seemed to think about it, cocking its head slightly as it looked at her. She found herself tugged by an emotion of curiosity, infecting her with a need to know more about this alien, just as it seemed to need the same from her.

"*Hyoo-munss,*" it hissed, curling a thin lip in a smile. It radiated a sense of being pleased with itself. It pointed to its bony chest again and spoke again. "*Kul-dar. Spec-terr,*" it hissed and pointed at the sitting human-cyborg.

The alien turned to Brandt and gestured at her, tapping a thin finger in the center of her chest with eyes full of question. Brandt fought the urge to step away, to move the hand away from her breasts, and even though she didn't move, the alien froze as though it sensed her discomfort. It did a strange thing, touching the fingertips of one hand to its forehead and closing its eyes as it gave a small bow, somehow conveying an apology directly into her feelings.

"Brandt," she said, touching her chest slightly higher up than the alien had been aiming for.

The alien smiled at her—the thin lips over the small mouth twitched and curled as though it was copying her own gesture.

"*Asha*," it said, placing a fingertip to its own breast and approximating a smile.

"Nice to meet you, Asha," Brandt said. "Do you need our help?"

Asha looked confused, glancing to Specter who watched for a sign that he was able to help. He turned to the plinth, kneeling down on long, thin legs and swiping away the little digital *Ichi* as fingers danced through the air and brought up a new hologram.

They leaned in closer, seeing a type of ship, but not by any design specifications they had ever seen.

The ship looked almost insectoid, with six articulated landing struts ending in spikes. The rear section of the ship was bulbous and seemed to be entirely engine. Protrusions from the small forward section bore the ominous look of heavy guns.

"What is that, Asha?" Brandt said. Acting on a hunch, she pointed at the holographic image and filled her thoughts and emotions with *curiosity*.

"*Va'alen*," he hissed. The word and his tone made them all feel a sense of dread and fear.

Brandt physically shuddered at the emotion that Asha projected. "Va'alen? They're another race? Aliens?"

"*Va'alen*," Asha repeated, giving them a secondary wave of fear and grief of loss.

If Brandt had to guess, she would assume that the Va'alen, whoever or whatever they were, had persecuted this race and this world. The ship certainly *looked* war-like.

Asha started speaking in his own language again, rattling clicks and rolling croaks filling the air. Brandt snatched the wrist device off her suit, scanning the occasional words of translation popping up on screen as the software worked hard to learn a new language in minutes.

War ... Invaded ... Destroyed technology ... Prisoners ... Patrol ... Twin suns.

Adding in the massive amounts of assumed detail, Brandt got the picture.

The Kuldar, Asha's people, were trapped on this planet. They lived under fear of discovery or invasion by the Va'alen, who patrolled the system and had something to do with the binary star system a few light years away.

This is heavy, she told herself. *Get a grip...*

"Show me the Va'alen," she said, pointing at the ship and trying to mime expanding the display. The large heads of the Kuldar seemed to hold a brain capable of more than their own, including the ability to communicate emotion. She was testing whether they had the ability to *read* emotion too. She thought about the ship she saw slowly rotating on the plinth, concentrating on her curiosity about the occupants.

Asha understood, swiping at the display and bringing up another holographic image that made all of them feel suddenly cold and afraid. Brandt doubted it was all from Asha projecting his own feelings.

The figure displayed stood beside a representation of a Kuldar for reference. It was a whole head taller, making the new figure almost two heads above a human. It was humanoid, with a secondary set of long upper limbs that ended in extended, curved claws. The claws looked deadly to anything not enclosed in armor.

Asha clicked a long rattle of his own words and Brandt looked down at her comm device's screen after tearing her eyes away from the beast on the holo-display. *Va'alen... male ... warrior caste ... kill.*

Brandt, as much as she tried to hide her feelings, had no desire whatsoever to meet one of them.

"Commander, come in," a voice emanated from the speaker in her comm device, snapping her back to the present and reminding her that Torres had been monitoring through her suit. He must have linked through Eze's suit after that. She smiled an apology at Asha who seemed to understand as she stepped back inside the armor and stayed still as it closed around her limbs and torso.

"Brandt," Torres said, "this isn't exactly what I had in mind for a first contact scenario…"

She glanced at the HUD icons, confirming that the link between the captain and her was a secure one.

"Me neither, sir," she said softly, trying to catch her breath after being in the lower oxygen environment. "What do we do?"

"Sit tight for now. Try and run the linguistic program with your new friend to build a language base for the translation software."

"Roger that, Captain," she replied. The connection was cut, no doubt for Torres to place a call home. They should know the team had inadvertently landed in the middle of an alien warzone.

"Ja—*Specter,* could you run a linguistic profile program with Asha?"

Specter nodded, ignoring her second slip-up. He detached the device from his own forearm to turn it around and show it to Asha.

The process for analyzing and translating a new language was an easy one. With any language on Earth it would only take about twenty minutes to learn an entirely new dialect and be able to translate that through a suit's software. The problem with using it on an alien planet was that every image it showed Asha was something new that he hadn't seen before: car, boat, cat, child, skyscraper. Each of these things was as weird and wonderful to him as the dark moss and stubby, black-leafed trees of his world were to them. His eyes widened at each unfamiliar image. The program ran for five minutes and had only picked up a few terms from him before Brandt shut it off.

"We'll need to find another way," she said.

"The file sent from Earth has downloaded now," Eze said. "Try now."

Specter tapped at the comm device and turned it back around to face Asha. The alien radiated delight at seeing his own language projected to him, then that elation suddenly stopped. He rattled off a rapid sequence of clicks at them, conveying a fearful anger as he spoke.

Where? ... my people ... ancient time ... legend.

"A ship crashed on our planet many years ago," Brandt said. "We think it must have come from here, from your people..."

Asha glanced at the comm device. It was working in both directions and translating some of Brandt's words into the hieroglyphs that he could read.

He spoke again, very few of his words translated to English, but he radiated the mixed feelings of fear, excitement and confusion. Brandt was saved from having to explain any more by the comm channel erupting into life.

"Contact, fast-moving," the comm officer onboard the *Ichi* barked. "Heading directly for the landing site. Scratch that, *two* fast-movers, you have *two* vessels incoming. LZ acknowledge."

Brandt heard the cool tones of Zero acknowledge the warning. He would have the few soldiers left under his command taking up defensive positions in readiness.

"Eze, stay here and guard Asha," she ordered. "Butler, external security and get your head on a swivel. Ja– *Specter*, on me."

Asha grew nervous as he heard the panic in the voices and felt the emotions of the humans. The female who seemed to be in charge said something that he didn't understand, but he felt that he should stay there and also that he should be afraid. He swiped at the plinth, bringing up a planetary image and highlighted the two red blips racing fast around the halo of habitable ground. They were flying directly toward where the humans had left their small ship. Those two blips were expanded by a command from his fingertips, enlarging to become the recognizable shapes of two small Va'alen patrol vessels.

The words of his wife, his queen, returned to him then with chilling intensity.

And if that message brings the Va'alen down on us, then there will be a reckoning for you.

CHAPTER 9

Proxima B Orbit

"Sir, you seeing these contacts?" the tactical officer asked Torres.

"Unfortunately, I am," he said. He had just seen the same type of ship on the display via Eze's suit. He hit the comm, calling Brandt. "Commander?"

"Here, sir." Her voice was strained as she ran hard across the soft, wet surface of the planet to reach the landing zone before the ships did. She knew they wouldn't make it; the trajectory displayed on her HUD showed their arrival time, and it was a full minute behind that of the two new ships.

"What are our chances that these new guys are willing to talk?" he asked.

"Between slim and none," she quipped back. "Any chance you can drop us a mech?"

Torres chewed at his lip as he considered the possibility of readying one of the two mechanized rigs they had onboard and getting it to the surface within a few minutes. Even as he thought, he knew it was pointless. There was no way to get them there without taking the *Ichi* in to land and endangering the entire mission.

"Sorry, Commander," he said. He hoped that her request wasn't the basis of an entire defensive plan.

"I know, sir," she said. "We have to deal with this—" She paused, an idea rapidly jumping into her head. "Sir, can the software patch for the turret controls be uploaded to the *Tanto*? Like, *RFN*?"

Torres looked at his tactical officer who nodded and began tapping at his screen.

"On it," Torres told Brandt. "I'll stay on the channel but leave you to do your thing."

"Roger that, sir." She thought of a million different things as she ran. A new icon flashed up on the top bar of her HUD for her authority to accept a remote software patch upload. She accepted it and called out to the LZ. "Zero, come in."

"Here. How long are we going to be on our own before you arrive?"

"A minute. Maybe two."

"Understood."

Zero turned to see two of the armored soldiers under his command already taking cover and readying spare magazines for their small carbines. Marcus, a big guy who looked every part the long-haul sailor, had wanted to take a squad support weapon but Zero had agreed with Brandt: going for a friendly first contact drop carrying an artillery piece didn't give off the right signals. He wished that the big guy had got his own way right now. He couldn't stop replaying the feed in his head about the Va'alen and their reputation for being big, aggressive assholes who liked to fill their spare time with long walks in the country and genocide.

Chopra, a close friend of Marcus but not half as big, nestled herself behind a wedge of low, smooth rocks the color of granite.

That's great, he thought to himself, *but what if they land behind you and come from the other direction?*

Any plan of action was better than inaction. Zero turned to the other two people at his LZ and was dismayed to see exactly that: inaction.

"Rogers!" he snapped at the pilot. "Get your ass strapped in and have this baby turning ready!"

"Sure you don't need the extra firepower?" Rogers patted the pistol on his thigh.

"You're likely to shoot yourself or me, fly-boy. Move your ass!"

Rogers fled up the ramp, and Byrne was left standing alone at the base of it. He was unsure what was expected of him and hoped he would receive a similar ass-chewing so that at least he knew what to do.

"If you wouldn't mind taking some cover and getting your weapon ready?" Zero enquired sarcastically. "You know, before the massive aliens turn up to rip your spine out and wear it like frikkin' jewelry?"

Byrne spun on the spot three times, finally seeing a depression of low ground and throwing himself into it. Zero alone stood out in the open, but he took the new marksman rifle off his back and checked that the magazine and the supercharger module were in place. He chambered a round and looked at the sky ready to face down with whatever landed.

Unclipping the mobile cover from the small of his back, he sighed to himself. "Bring it on."

~

"Comm: get me Earth on subspace now," Torres snapped. He didn't have time to move to the briefing room or his private cabins to place the call. The screen sprang to life and the surprised look on the female commander's face told him how unorthodox his transmission was.

"No time, Commander," he snapped. "I know you don't want to tell me if and when we are expecting additional fleet resources in this system, but we could do with them immediately." She opened her mouth to respond, but Torres wasn't finished and wasn't in the mood for a conversation. "We have made first contact with a friendly and intelligent alien race, but we now have a contact with *another* alien race and our intel shows them to be far from friendly. We do not know their weapon or combat capabilities, but we are about to find out the hard way very soon. If you have help available," he finished loudly, "then please… send it now."

"Zero, Grip. ETA ninety seconds. Copy?"

The radio blared in his ear, but Zero didn't hear the words.

Instead he watched as what looked like two fat bees came into focus, flying in perfect synchronicity as they weaved toward the LZ, switching in and out of one another's path.

"Stand by," he said in a hoarse voice. "We got incoming."

The two ships were both about the same size as the *Tanto* in the main body, but seemed taller and larger by their insectoid legs of landing gear that bored deep holes into the soft moss as they settled down to land. Even their ships seemed to lean down and intimidate as the engines whined down to near silence. The forward sections of the ships were reflective and black with a honeycomb pattern, much like the insect eyes they reminded him of. Gun barrels protruded from the fuselage, and he swallowed hard as a hissing noise came from the nearest ship. The forward section lifted up and over, terribly, slowly, to reveal a hideous sight. Zero watched, holding his breath.

The thing stood, rising from its chair before stepping out into thin air ahead of Zero to land heavily ten paces in front of them. It crouched slightly on landing, but then stood to its full height and stretched out its spine to show its huge size.

Standing over eight feet tall on thick, gnarled and knotted muscular legs, it stretched all four of its arms out wide and rotated its head to look at Zero, who suddenly felt so small and not at all dangerous.

Not head, Zero thought as he tried to find some way to describe what he was seeing. *That isn't a head, it's more like a helmet or something.*

There was no mouth, no discernable features of the thing and no obvious articulation between body and head like the humans' fragile-looking necks. To turn and look sideways, which it did when the almost identical but slightly smaller creature dropped from the front section of the other ship, the thing had to turn its whole upper body, all four arms moving with it.

The two aliens seemed to make visual contact with each other, then both turned back to look at him.

"Err, hi?" Zero said. The aliens made no response.

"We are from Earth," Zero said, his words loud and spoken slowly. His tone tried to sound friendly, but the grip on his rifle stayed firm. Still they made no move to show that they had heard or understood him.

"Umm, Commander?" Zero said quietly into his comm. "You, uh..." He chuckled nervously. "You far away?"

The two aliens snapped their focus up and away from him to face the treeline behind. Their two right hands reached behind them and came back with fat, bulbous pods that were unmistakably weapons from the way they were held, implying an obviously dangerous business end.

The first noises the new creatures had made rumbled out, low and powerful, and both scattered left and right for the cover of their ships' landing struts in another coordinated move. Zero instinctively dove for the small cover provided by the *Tanto*.

"Don't fire! Don't fire!" Brandt shouted. She stepped into the clearing that was their LZ and held her hands out to show open palms. "Let's just…" She swallowed, seeing the sheer size and menacing figure of a Va'alen up close for the first time. "Let's just be nice…"

She stepped forward, arms still held out to show that she meant no harm. She hoped that the aliens could tell she meant no harm and saw the one that had been towering over Zero fix on her directly.

It seemed to be looking at her. She couldn't say for sure if it was, because the face was featureless and shiny, but she got the distinct impression that she was now its main focus.

Its target.

"Human people," a metallic growl announced startling them all, "should not come to this place."

They all froze, trying to fathom how their language was being spoken by these beasts unknown to them an hour before.

"Human people," a slightly higher-pitched metallic growl said, "go now, and forget Kuldar hiding. We kill them now."

Brandt paused briefly before answering. "We can't do that."

The larger Va'alen roared a deafening challenge, rising up to its terrifying full height and swinging the fat gun up into a four-handed firing pose. Nothing they had ever seen before made the same noise or fired the same way. A flash of orange light seared from the barrel and launched a bolt of energy across the clearing aimed directly at the exposed ground commander.

A dozen things happened at once. Specter, his superhuman reflexes already propelling him toward Brandt before she had even fully registered what was happening, slammed into her as he simultaneously activated his personal shield generator.

The bolt of energy hit him and dissipated against his protective shield. In doing so, it transferred the energy kinetically to send both of them flying away at a hard angle. They hit the trees, flying through the first layer of dense, black foliage and snapping off branches as they tumbled to the ground, digging furrows in the soft moss.

"Are you okay?" Specter asked, scanning her suit for signs of damage.

"Cosmetic," she said as her HUD reported no major system malfunctions. "Go."

The sounds of gunfire had already begun in the clearing.

Zero ran a fast lap around the *Tanto* to pop up on the other side of the small craft and bring his rifle to bear. He knew what a dozen well-placed rounds could do with the new, fully charged rifle in skilled hands—his were definitely skilled. He couldn't acquire the first one, the one that had fired and done who-knew-what damage to his teammates. The other, however, was still taking cover behind the landing strut of its ship and it showed its entire exposed left flank to Zero and his weapon.

"Smile, asshole," he muttered. They were humanoid in appearance, he reminded himself. They walked upright on two legs despite the extra set of arms; there would have to be a nervous system running from the main control center to the extremities. That control center would certainly be the head. He pulled the trigger with the target reticule hovering over the base of the creature's head.

Three rounds left the barrel of his gun, all heavy caliber and all supercharged by the singularity device seated ahead of the trigger guard.

Instantly, three corresponding bullet holes blossomed in the creature's thick shell-like hide which, had it been human, would have removed the entire upper section of its spinal column.

It stopped firing, spinning to acquire him in a heartbeat as it switched the bulbous gun from its right hand claws to the two left ones.

Four arms and ambidextrous? Zero thought. *Not fair!*

He threw himself out of the line of sight, yelling into the comm for Rogers to raise the shields on the *Tanto* to full. He hit the button just in time as two, three, four rapid bolts of orange energy projectiles seared the dull, red light of their battle ground and rocked the small ship on its landing struts. Trapped inside the shield bubble, and temporarily safe, Zero watched in horror as the thing ran low at him and slammed its body into the shield. It bounced back, struck an animalistic pose of intimidation, and let out a roar that he could hear over the gunfight. As it turned, full of impotent rage, he saw the three clear holes his gun had made beginning to close up.

"Center mass," he called into the comm as he stared in horror. "Aim for center mass."

Marcus rose from his position of cover and emptied a full magazine into the right side of the creature.

Fight with what you have, he reminded himself. What he had was a kickass new carbine that fired the god of all known armor-piercing rounds. The problem, unfortunately, was that their technology was dominant only in their world, and they weren't in their world any longer.

The gun clicked dry and he fumbled for a replacement magazine to fit. It may be kickass, but his muscle-memory was not yet attuned to the new weapon. Raising his eyes again, Marcus saw that his last seventy rounds, almost all of them on target, had gained the unwelcome and undivided attention of the huge beetle-like thing headed straight for him. Racking back the charging handle, he aimed and emptied the second magazine into the advancing alien.

Chopra, not hitting her target with as many rounds either, watched the beast change direction and head directly at Marcus. She raised herself to one knee and added her fire to his, hoping to bring it down together like a pair of big game hunters. Behind her, spurred into a mad dash of bravery or stupidity, came Byrne from behind their ship.

He was running, closing the distance between him and the creature to enhance the effects of concentrated small arms fire. Three paces before he reached it, foolishly yelling a battle cry in rage and fear, the thing turned and backhanded him with both left hands. Byrne was knocked back down to the soft ground with a thud. Deep scratches had been scored across the chest of his armor with the curved claws of both hands. The creature continued to soak up intense fire from two fronts, but this nearest threat had angered it. It reached down, grabbing Byrne's left leg in one powerful claw, and swung him by the ankle to smash his body into Marcus's. The huge man was knocked down and the gun shattered in his hands.

With one fewer attacker to defend against, it turned to acquire the next target. As it cocked back an arm to launch the limp, metal body it held, a new wave of incoming rounds battered its thick carapace.

Zero called for the shields on the *Tanto* to drop and allow him to re-join the fight. Emerging from the edge of the trees, Specter drilled bullet after supercharged bullet into the shoulder of the alien arm holding their comrade. His shots were accurate beyond normal human ability; the concentration of fire was so acute that the limb suffered enough damage to compel it to drop the man. The arm hung limply beside the armored carapace of its huge, insect-like body. It dropped Byrne, turned to face the new onslaught and raised the gun with its still undamaged arms. The gun fired, and Specter threw himself to the side for the shot to pass him harmlessly by. He leapt through the air, slamming both feet onto the damaged shoulder of the thing and severing the destroyed limb. He drew his weapons and fired relentlessly in the hope that he could drill a hole through the hard, armored skin of the beast.

The shot from the alien rifle that had missed Specter found another mark by pure, random, terrible chance. Brandt had risen with difficulty, resetting some of her suit's systems after the massive impact had jarred her. Just as she reached running speed and entered the clearing again she was thrown down hard, spinning to her right in a wild movement she couldn't arrest, until she came to a stop hard against a wide, soft tree trunk.

Ahead of her she could see Chopra and Zero engaging the creature farthest away, could see its body rocking and rippling with the impacts of bullets. Even under such an attack, it seemed to feel no pain. She saw Specter standing on the downed body of the other one, the muzzle of his carbine alive with flame as he fired relentlessly at point blank range. He reached for a replacement magazine as his gun stopped firing.

Brandt couldn't move. Couldn't raise her own weapon to aid any of her team. The servos of her suit had been scrambled by the energy blast and her physical strength wasn't enough to force the unpowered suit to articulate. All she had was the menu system, and she tried the last thing she could to save them all.

CHAPTER 10

Near Proxima Centauri

"Contact, eighteen thousand kilometers," shouted the tactical officer on the bridge of the *Ichi*.

"Talk to me," Torres said.

"Sir, they're squawking UN ident codes. It's the *Hammer* from the colony fleet."

Torres relaxed at this news. His heart had dropped through his guts at the prospect of this new ship being more of the hostile aliens that his friends were battling on the surface.

"Second contact, twelve thousand clicks. It's the *Venture*, Captain."

"Call 'em up," Torres said as he took his seat again. "Put it on screen."

~

"Jump complete, Admiral. The *Hammer* is here... and so is another ship. It's the recon ship, sir, the *Boken sha*."

"The *Ichi*," Dassiova corrected him.

"They're hailing us."

"On screen," Dassiova said, taking his seat as the strong, good-looking features of a youthful man appeared on the wall.

"Sir," Torres said hurriedly, "no time to explain fully, but I need your ships to adopt defensive positions around the planet we're orbiting. I have a ground team in contact with hostile alien forces."

"Understood, Captain. Helm, bring us into orbit and deploy weapons systems," Dassiova said as he hit the ship-wide comm channel to activate it. "All hands, battle stations. Battle stations." He turned to the comm officer and gave his orders. "Signal the *Hammer*. My compliments to Captain Hayes; he is to push out a perimeter and protect the ships in orbit. And I want our ground teams on standby ready to deploy as soon as we're in position."

The admiral sat back, adrenaline coursing through his veins as he wished for nothing more than to pick up a rifle and mix it with whoever—*what*ever—threatened his people.

"Sir, we have multiple contacts," shouted the excitable tactical officer.

"Understood. On screen," Captain Hayes told her, biting down the urge to shush her. The viewscreen came to life, showing nothing but the empty blackness of space tinged a dull red on one side. "I don't see anything, tactical." Professional annoyance sharpened his words.

"I don't understand, Captain," she said as she tapped furiously at the screen. "These coordinates are exactly where the contacts registered."

"Wait," called out the helmsman from his pilot position below the big display. "Light distortion… *there*. You see it?"

"Okay people," Captain Hayes said as he stood and paced his bridge. As he walked, he stroked the small goatee he had grown to cover the scar earned in one of his many clashes with terrorist factions on Earth. "We are facing off against hostile alien forces utilizing some kind of distortion or"—he shuddered at the use of the word—"*cloaking* technology. Tac? Give them a burst of fire directly across the path of the lead contact, see if that doesn't change their minds."

The massive pair of chain guns whirred to life and chattered their destructive noise to the coordinates where the cloaked ship would be. They watched on screen as the luminous tracer rounds—irradiated to shine bright green, like glow sticks—rippled into the distortion magnified on the display.

A collective gasp went around the bridge. Only Hayes stayed silent, despite his brain screaming at him from behind his mask of cool command. The rippling image flickered, unveiling whatever distortion field had masked their visual signature. It revealed not one contact but four. As one, they turned towards the *Hammer* and opened fire with searing bolts of orange energy. Discovering three other contacts meant that Hayes's frigate was facing twelve of the alien ships in addition to the four already inside weapons range.

"All guns: weapons-free, *weapons-free*," he called out confidently as he turned to the tactical officer. "Tac? Drop me two singularity warheads into the path of each of the other readings. Do it now." He was rocked forward, bumping into her as he steadied himself and told her again to fire the goddamned warheads.

The bridge shook again, their entire ship rocked by impacts and disrupting their grav-field.

"Shields down to eighty-one percent, Captain," the second tactical officer reported.

"Boost auxiliary banks to shield array," he said, wondering how anything could take almost a fifth of his ship's shields offline in just one pass. Everything on Earth, singularity weapons notwithstanding, would bounce off like kids throwing rocks at a dropship. "I want th—"

A huge, resounding *boom* of an explosion silenced him as the tremor of the impact vibrated through his whole body.

"Two targets down," tactical shouted. "Second one just took a dive into our port flank. Port shields at sixty-eight percent."

"We can't take hits like that all day," Hayes growled. "Have we got every gun firing?"

"Yes, sir," an officer called out.

Another round of resonating small booms rippled up from his boots through the captain's legs.

"Ventral shields took a major hit, sir. We're getting chewed up out here!"

Hayes had no time to tell that crewman to get a grip on himself before another report fired back at him.

"Warheads detonated; two targets down but one more incoming."

"On screen," he ordered again, wanting to see the enemy who was carving up his well-armed frigate with their swarm of smaller ships.

Sixteen goddamned ships, he thought sourly. *The Hammer is not going to fall to a handful of alien pirates...*

"Target down," called the woman from tactical. "Five remaining."

Hayes looked at the screen. It looked like a big bug from one of the many hot swamps he had been in during his career with the UNPF.

He watched as one broke off from the mini swarm of three and headed straight for the viewfinder linked to his screen. It wasn't running a collision course straight at him, but it sure as hell felt like it.

"Bring us about," he ordered the helm. "Plot a half-second jump back toward our original insertion point."

The helmsman hesitated, glancing at the navigation and comm officers who shared his horror.

"Do it now, crewman," Hayes ordered, sitting back down in his chair and setting a grim look on his face.

"Hit it!"

~

Admiral Dassiova ignored the verbal reports from his large bridge crew, instead electing to block out the non-essential external sounds and concentrate on interpreting the display beside him. He saw the *Hammer*, its shield strength readings showing in simple and—worryingly—rapidly declining digits. He saw, in the left margin, the ammo reserves of the guns also ticking down as almost every cannon chattered away on full-auto at the multiple attackers buzzing around it. He watched the big ship spin fast; maneuvering thrusters on the front and back on each side firing together to slew the massive space tank around on the spot so that it pointed directly back toward the enemy.

Dassiova saw the number of enemy on the display, saw how fast the shields were being degraded, and knew exactly what Hayes was about to do.

He was bringing their knives to the *Venture*'s gunfight.

"Shields to maximum," he ordered. "Turn us about: one hundred degrees starboard, order all guns to stand ready."

Nobody hesitated. His orders were obeyed before the *Hammer* vanished from the display. He worried for a moment if he had been correct in ordering the *Norton* to stay behind and guard the *Cortez* in deep space. The *Hammer* was getting badly beat up without her sister ship to bounce off. He pushed that thought away, snapping his fingers as he pointed to a comm officer.

"Signal the *Norton* on subspace; tell them to jump in immediately and come out swinging with everything they have."

"Sir, the *Hammer* has jumped back toward us!" the tactical officer cried out.

"I'm aware of that," Dassiova said patiently. "Open warhead bays and prepare to target the enemy ships."

The five remaining ships had now become nine with the arrival of a further two cloaked pods. They were heading straight for the beleaguered half a fleet in orbit over a firefight on the surface that was all but over.

~

Brandt could barely breathe. The heavy plate of her armor restricted her limbs without power to the movement servos. All she could do was take small breaths and move her eyes over the menu commands.

Her HUD told her that Byrne and Marcus were still alive, but both were flashing warning triangles above their icons.

She didn't know if either of them—hell if *any* of them— were going to make it back alive. Just as the furthest monster away found its target and churned up the earth and rock around Chopra, the creature under the boots of Specter landed a clawed hook hard against his abdomen. His whole body flashed electric blue as the personal shield that was built into him absorbed the kinetic energy.

But energy always had to go somewhere, and in this case, it flung him through the air. He spun wildly and lost his primary weapon, before hitting the ground hard three paces from where Zero was rapidly pulling the trigger of his battle rifle. The marksman's attention was drawn to the hideous creature that rose up, one limp arm dangling lifelessly by a single, stubborn sinew. Its battered body oozed a black, oily substance from the mess of bullet wounds that had penetrated the thick carapace. With the two remaining good hands on one side it raised its gun and took aim at Specter.

Zero faced a terrible choice. Beside him was a very valuable soldier; a remarkable machine worth a handful of regular troops in battle. Ahead of him, under increasing fire, Chopra faced death in seconds if he couldn't turn the tide of attack away from her.

He tried to save both of them.

Keeping the rifle pulled in close to his shoulder, Zero released the grip with his left hand and reached behind his back to snatch the mobile cover device.

He tossed it just past Specter who was struggling to regain his feet and watched as three rapid-fired bolts of orange energy hit the shield. The percentage readout flashed a warning on his HUD: it was already at only fifty-six percent. He hoped that the few seconds and the two salvos of alien fire that the cover would give Specter would be enough for him to get back in the fight or get to safety. His rate of fire had lessened as he did this, but as he turned around he saw that those precious heartbeats spent trying to do two things at once had given their enemy the advantage.

Bulbous, alien gun held low in one of the right hands, the farthest insectoid alien rose up over Chopra. The lower hand on the other side swatted away the short barrel of her carbine. The two free hands, the higher ones with longer reach and more curved claws, towered over the soldier ready to drive down and skewer her through her armored torso.

Both descending hook-clawed arms disintegrated, as a savage and deafening burst of heavy gunfire filled the clearing. It wasn't gunfire like they were used to. It was the big ship-to-ship ordnance that was far too heavy and destructive to deploy against a person.

~

Brandt pushed the concern that she was paralyzed out of her mind. It was just the threat of panic causing her pulse to quicken. She also knew, logically, that she couldn't move her limbs because the suit's power module running the armor's articulation servos was damaged, but that didn't stop her having those thoughts.

Using the only thing she could move, her eyes, she accessed the software patch that had been downloaded to her suit.

Grateful that the main power and the wireless uplink systems were undamaged, she activated the remote-control program for the *Tanto*'s main guns.

Inside the protected ship, yelling uselessly into his comm, Rogers found himself inexplicably locked out of the weapons control system. He watched in stunned awe as the gun display burst into life on his main screen and began to rotate without a single command from him.

Brandt used her eyes to control the quad turret of heavy slugs designed to pass through the *Tanto*'s own shielding and batter away at an enemy ship's protective barrier. They were of a caliber that none of the ground troops had ever used, even in the heavy mech rigs that could bring down a dropship with their auto-cannons.

Their own weapons, even with the revolutionary armor-piercing capabilities of the singularity charge, were ineffective. They were designed to beat everything created by humanity. Any man-made armor or shielding could be defeated by their new technology. But even this tech was pointless and inadequate against the armor and weapons possessed by these aliens.

The huge, beetle-like humanoid bodies of these hostile creatures with their war-like tendencies were equal to twenty, maybe even thirty, fully armed human soldiers. These were the most dangerous adversaries anyone from Earth had ever encountered.

The chain gun protruding from the outer hull of the *Tanto* spun up; a shrieking, metallic whine pierced their thoughts as the triangular barrels whipped around to start firing the big slugs at the target. Brandt watched as though from outside her own body. Centering the crosshairs on the creature about to attack her soldier, she disabled the safety program and narrowed her eyes to pull the virtual trigger.

With a crack and a thud, the first huge projectiles spat from the gun and tore the air to the target in a millisecond. The fifteen heavy slugs, each charged with a dose of singularity energy capable of running an automobile for twenty miles, left the barrel in the first second of firing and obliterated the raised arms of the alien. All four limbs were shattered and blown away from the grotesque body in an instant as the thing rocked and spasmed under the onslaught. Three of the slugs tore great holes straight through the torso and toppled it; its rigid body fell backward like a tree as it noiselessly collapsed.

The gun had stopped firing and the silence ended with the soft thump of the downed beast hitting the mossy ground.

The other one bellowed; a cry of pure, animalistic anguish and rage as it forgot the team it was trying to kill. It crouched low, springing through the air to fly twenty paces and land beside the limp, limbless body of the other.

Reaching down with two of its remaining three working arms, it scooped up the huge carcass with effortless ease and sprang forward again, losing the dangling limb in the process. It landed back inside the open cockpit of its ship. That cockpit door closed, and the engines began to shriek and whine as the curious leg-like landing gear rose.

Brandt tracked the ship with the guns protruding from the roof of the *Tanto* but didn't fire. They had done enough.

"Everybody…" she murmured with labored breathing. "Everybody sound off…"

"Zero," her marksman groaned. "Byrne is dead. Marcus is badly injured. Specter's banged up and Chopra's okay. Physically. Where the hell are you?"

"Trees," she muttered.

Brandt blinked off the override controls for the guns and imagined that she could hear them powering down and retracting. She could make out her surroundings again and trusted in the HUD's software to give them a bearing on her paralyzed location. She saw the red outline of Zero's suit fifty paces ahead and to her left, and talked him toward her so that he could use his own powered armor to lift hers. Specter had regained his feet, having to reset a number of his systems before he was functional once more. He set Marcus's armor into life-preservation mode. This had locked the entire suit into the position he had fallen in to prevent any movement of his neck and back. Once this had been locked, Specter helped Chopra carry him back to the ship

"We need to get Byrne's body," Brandt told them as she was rested inside the shuttle.

"I'll get him," Specter said, his left cheek twitching rapidly under the eye. "You stay there."

"Funny, asshole," she quipped back at him. She wouldn't be going anywhere unless someone managed to power-up her suit or activate the emergency release feature.

Specter paused, looking like he was about to say something, but instead turned back to walk outside. He returned a minute later carrying the limp form of Byrne and set him down on the deck of the *Tanto*. He ran back out again and returned holding the severed arm of the monster he had tried to amputate with bullets, setting the long, bony limb down carefully as though it still posed a danger.

"Close it up," he yelled as he thumped the bulkhead twice with his robotic hands.

Rogers didn't answer, except to raise the ramp and cycle up the engines. This lifted them off the mossy ground and took them back out to space where the promise of medical attention awaited.

"Viper, Grip," Brandt said weakly into her comm. Specter started work on manually overriding her suit's release function.

"Here, Commander," she replied somberly. "We saw the contact. Asha says this is common for the Va'alen to patrol in their mating pairs. I think that is what he says, but he says that where there are two, there are always two more. He says they are like a storm."

"A storm or a swarm?" Brandt asked. "Because we got our asses handed to us by just two of them… Sit tight, we'll be back for you just as soon as we can. And no joyriding in the alien ship left here, okay?"

106

CHAPTER 11

Proxima B Orbit

"Captain," Dassiova said to Torres, "I'd recommend you place yourselves to our starboard and out of our line of fire. Dassiova out."

"Good to see you again, Admiral," Torres replied to the closed comm channel in sarcastic retort. He didn't need that particular order reiterated to him. He nodded at his helmsman to get them on the safe side of the fifty guns.

"ETA on the *Tanto* getting back to us?" he asked the bridge officers. The short delay in their response flashed anger behind his eyes. He quickly mastered it to prevent his façade from cracking.

While Torres was attempting to mask his annoyance that nobody had given him the answer, the comm officer hailed them to ask for their estimate. It should have been the tactical officer's job to know the trajectory of an incoming ship, but given that there were seventeen of them showing on the three-dimensional display, Torres had to let it slide. He had bigger things on his mind.

"Sir," the comm officer told him, "*Tanto* reports seven minutes to docking bay. They have three injured and one... they have one KIA sir."

"Understood," Torres said gravely. He felt the stinging blow of failure in his command since he had lost a member of his crew after mere days at sea. He knew he would have to deal with that later, but for now he needed to get his people back onboard and deal with the ever-advancing threat of the small ships burning hard towards them. "Put us off the starboard bow of the…" he looked at the display to see the ident code of the gargantuan colony ship commanded by his old commander and now his admiral, "…the *Venture* and face us directly away from the enemy's advance."

"Sir?" the helmsman asked, confused by his logic.

"Did I stutter, helm?"

"Sir, no sir," the officer said, working the controls to move the *Ichi* to the selected position.

"Tactical? ETA on those enemy ships to weapons range?" "Seven minutes, sir…" he reported.

"Comm? Signal the *Tanto* to come in low to avoid the field of fire. Tell them we expect them about the same time as enemy contact so *not* to get their asses in the middle of anything."

The comm officer acknowledged him.

Torres activated the ship's intercom from his chair. "Gunners, this is the captain. Stand by to engage the enemy at close quarters. I anticipate that they will look to loop the *Venture* for a flanking attack and use her size against her. We will be ready for that and pick off anything that tries to hug her hull. Torres out.

"Tactical? Did you have a chance to analyze their movement and attack patterns from their clash with the *Hammer*?"

"Yes, sir," came the stressed but confident reply. "They work in two pairs primarily; each pair of ships mirroring the other like they're synchronized. Their flight patterns aren't too erratic, but they seem to vary acceleration constantly, so it's difficult to get a lead on them unless they come head-on."

"It strikes me that they have little choice after whoever is running that frigate had the sense and balls to jump her back this way," Torres said, leaning back slightly to get comfortable in the six remaining minutes before things got noisy.

Their viewscreen, still activated, now blacked out as the dull, red glow from the small star was masked entirely by the enormous ship that now shadowed them. Torres waited, feeling the urge to say or do something building up inside him like a volcano. He held back. Letting it out would reveal his youth and inexperience in the chair. He never would have been in it were it not for the sequence of randomly violent events that led them to flee the surface of the moon only weeks before. The silence stretched out, marked only by the minutes ticking down to combat that were called out by his tactical officer.

"Sir," the tactical officer said with a wavering voice, "I'm picking up three more contacts."

He gave a bearing that would place this new threat approaching side-on to the three ships; one huge, one small and one limping and damaged. Torres checked that the other ships were aware of the fact. He asked for a comm link to Dassiova onboard the *Venture,* which was fed to the small terminal beside his chair.

"Admiral, where do you need us?" he said, getting right to the point.

"Just sit tight, Captain," Dassiova told him. "We've got a little more up our sleeves just yet. *Venture* out."

Torres furrowed his brow, trying to figure out what the stone-faced admiral could mean by that before his thoughts were interrupted by another announcement.

"*Tanto* slowing for approach," he was told, "and the *Venture* has opened fire on the incoming vessels."

Torres instinctively tilted his head to try and hear the sounds of the guns firing. He knew that the black void beyond their hull and shield could hold no sound, knew that the vacuum of space would be showing a silent movie of the huge gunfight, but the human part of him that could not be turned off still tried to use its senses like he was still in his natural environment on Earth.

~

"Don't wait for my order," Dassiova said. "You damn well launch the second they are in range and can't evade our warheads."

"Aye aye, sir," the other officer at the tactical station answered. "Launching warheads on my mark... *mark*."

The ship vibrated with deep thudding noises as missile after missile ignited inside their launch tubes and seared away through the inky-black expanse towards the insect-like vessels coming for them.

Eighteen sleek, black missiles streaked out of the port side launchers. They disappeared from view in an instant, lost in the shining expanse of emptiness with only the glow of their propulsion vents giving away their presence. The weapons were small, their heavy ordnance powered by their own warheads. This made them harder to detect without state-of-the art sensor systems.

To their credit, whoever these hostile and unknown aliens were, they identified the incoming missiles. Only the first of the four clusters of ships was destroyed by the growing ripple of a collapsing singularity. The other clusters split apart and took evasive maneuvers in their pairs to begin their individual attack runs against the huge targets.

It was a battle of agility versus size. Maneuverability against might. The massive guns of the *Venture* chattered and droned as they spat their heavy projectiles at the attacking ships. The targeting systems computed to work out their patterns and tactics. The guns gave the ships a long lead, aiming ahead and trying to anticipate where they were going to be in the twenty or so seconds it would take for the ships and the munitions to travel the huge distances.

The officer on the tactical station watched this unfolding, predicted the patterns in the data that rolled across his terminal, and gave his best guess to the admiral.

"Sir, they are working in pairs. I suggest concentrating all fire on one or two ships at once to cover all possible evasive options; better to pick them off one by one than spend all da —" He stopped as the ship rocked.

The bridge officer beside him call out the percentage reduction in their main shields.

"Suicide run, hold on a second… Sir, if we shoot down one of the pairs then the other turns kamikaze on us. I think."

"Call out the targets," Dassiova barked. "Any of them look like they're taking a suicide run at us, I want all fire concentrated on them. Pick one off, then wait for their partner to come straight at us."

His orders were followed and started to show some success. "Target down!"

"Incoming bomb run, bearing…"

The tide of battle was going in their favor. The *Venture* lost

less than five percent capacity of its shields for each ship they destroyed.

"Sir, those new incoming targets are approaching weapons range."

Dassiova took pause, hoping that the timing of his other frigate captain would be… *heroic.* It wasn't, and he gave an order that he knew could be very costly to the lives of the brave men and women under his command.

"Signal Captain Hayes on the *Hammer*," he said solemnly. "Order him to block their approach."

"But, sir," the comm officer said, "they've sustained heavy damage and are down to thirty percent shields…" She stopped talking as her eyes met the admiral's. "Yes, sir," she finished.

He knew the facts.

Dassiova heard Hayes's acknowledgment, heard the heavy tone of acceptance as the captain of the frigate prepared to spend his life and lives of his crew to save the fleet. The admiral watched as the icon for the *Hammer* moved into a blocking position almost four thousand kilometers off their bow. Dassiova was afraid to look away, but more afraid to watch the sacrifice of so many men and women laying down their lives to protect the fleet flagship and its commander.

⁓

"*Tanto*'s eight hundred kilometers off, sir," the tactical officer on the bridge of the *Ichi* reported. "*Contact, coming fast from the planet!*"

Torres looked in shock at the single enemy ship blinking on the screen. He didn't need a trajectory report to see what was happening: it was on a collision course with their shuttle. He had seen the destruction their suicide runs had wrought on the *Venture* and how they had mercilessly shredded the shields of the *Hammer*. He knew in an instant the *Tanto* wouldn't survive a hit like that.

Weighing the risk to the crew against the certainty of losing everyone onboard the smaller ship, he ordered the helm to initiate a full burn on an intercept course.

"Guns, hit that thing with everything we have; concentrate all fire on that ship."

As the vibration of the firing guns became a dull thrum felt through the bulkheads and decks of the ship, it was a race against time.

Almost five thousand kilometers away on the bridge of the *Hammer*, Captain Hayes addressed his crew. He kept it short and to the point. He told them knew they would all do their duty with their last breath and reminded them that they all had a job to do. Right then, right now, that job was making sure that those incoming ships could not get past them and attack the *Venture*.

"*Gimme everything you've got,*" he whispered to his ship as he settled back into his chair. "*Atta girl...* Damage teams stand by. All guns: weapons free." He raised his voice. "Give the bastards hell."

"It's the ship from the surface," Rogers yelled over his shoulder. The vibrations inside the little ship made it hard to hear. "It's comin' in fast. Hold on; I need to take evasive maneuvers."

He gave them no time to react to the warning, no time to secure their straps before he threw the miniature version of its mothership into a twisting roll and a sudden, spinning dive. He then drastically changed direction and forced the pursuing craft to adjust speed and course. The gravity emitter, despite being turned up, did nothing to hold them down. The maneuvers threw the exhausted contents of the rear section around, sounding like tools left in a tumble drier. Specter held tight to the grab handles and wedged his feet against the bulkhead. He pressed his cybernetic body into the locked frame of Marcus's armor to prevent any more danger to the man's life than his horrific injuries already did.

Brandt, now free from her armor after Specter had managed to manually crank open her suit's release mechanism, bounced hard off the armored shoulder of Zero. She then hit the deck flat on her back driving the air from her lungs.

That's gonna leave a mark, she complained to herself pointlessly.

Rogers righted the small ship, levelling it out and punching it so hard that they all felt the shove backward and instinctively fought against it.

As soon they had adjusted to the inertia of hard acceleration, they had to stop themselves from pitching forward toward the cockpit when Rogers switched to a hard stop. Anyone not strapped in risked flying out into space via the bulkhead in front of the pilot.

Momentary weightlessness, courtesy of their grav emitter that could barely keep up, followed as Rogers pitched them into another steep dive.

"Commander," the pilot yelled in a tone somewhere between unimaginable panic and professional concentration, "I could *really* use your trick with the guns again."

Brandt's eyes settled on the pieces of her armor skating around the deck of the passenger bay. She wouldn't be able to replicate that particular show any time soon. Her eyes caught Zero's; he shook his visored head to say that he didn't have the software patch to use them.

"I'll do it manually," she said, fighting her way forward to the cockpit and the vacant co-pilot's seat.

"Not at these velocities you won't," Rogers told her. "At this range they're moving just too damned fast for us to get a shot off and—*Dammit!*" He cursed as a series of bright orange streaks flashed ahead of them. Their pursuer had fired a burst.

"Commander, I have *no* idea what will happen outside of atmosphere if these assholes hit us with their god-damned ray guns."

Just as Brandt opened her mouth to respond, a huge impact rocked them and blackened the interior of the ship in a terrifying instant. The artificial gravity failed, as did their engines, shields and life support. They tumbled through the blackness. Only the soldiers still encased in working armor retained much in the way of their wits, since the HUDs provided them some information. Rogers and Brandt, arguably the two most important people onboard the small ship, were spun around in total darkness with no concept of which way was up; Brandt, because her useless armor had been discarded on the deck and now floating free, and Rogers because he was not used to having armor, and hadn't activated the helmet.

"We need to reset the systems manually," Specter shouted over the sounds of the contents of their ship crashing around. "The electronics have tripped, so we're not quite dead in the water yet."

"Access panel," Rogers yelled through gritted teeth. He tried to keep the contents of his stomach inside. "Deck under the jump seat. Manual override for maintenance."

Specter said nothing. He clamped his impossibly strong robotic hand onto the grab rail and leaned back to pull open the maintenance hatch underneath the seat nearest the hangar door.

"Pump it… three times to… prime it first," Rogers cried, the G-forces exerted on his brain threatening to black him out at any second.

"Hurry, Jake," Brandt added, just as her own mind went fuzzy.

CHAPTER 12

Proxima B

"Open fire!" Torres shouted. The stress and over-excitement of the move made his voice sound far louder than a captain should use to give his orders. The four gun bubbles of the *Ichi* rattled and chirped as their triangular barrels, like the gun system on the *Tanto*, burst into life and poured fire into the oncoming path of the ship that had just shot down his team. They had concentrated their fire to cover the whole area the alien ship was heading for, and their saturation of that tiny part of space with charged projectiles paid in full.

There was no explosion, no boiling fireball to mark the destruction of their enemy, only the sparking of the dying power as wires and metal were torn apart when the ship broke up into pieces, The bits continued to plough their sparking way onward through space without slowing. Further parts of the bulbous craft disintegrated as the damage caused the parts of it still pressurized to come apart. Soon none of the debris left was large enough to contain anything still living.

"Target destroyed," reported the tactical officer. The other officers watched the destruction in full screen on the bridge's main display.

"Sir, incoming comm from the *Tanto*. Audio only," called out the comm officer.

"On speaker," Torres ordered. He retook his seat with more dignity than when he had leapt out of it like a sports fan with money riding on the outcome of a single play.

"*Boken sha Ichi*, this is Specter, how copy?" came the crackling voice.

Torres recognized the voice, recognized the callsign of their ghostly secret crewmember. The weak signal was due to the transmission coming from a suit and not automatically rebroadcast through the ship systems as it normally would have been.

"Specter, *Ichi* Actual, you're coming in *two-by-three*," Torres told him.

"Captain," came the muffled but familiar voice back at him. He spoke slowly and clearly like he was giving instructions to an unruly child. "We have been hit, bandit is still out there, I have restored basic power, but I cannot, I repeat, I *cannot* get the ship back to you. Copy?"

"Copy that, Specter. Be advised your bandit is no more. Stand by." Torres clicked on a separate communication channel and got Doctor Paterson in the main lab.

"Paterson, have you or Harris got any tricks up your sleeves for retrieving our little bird which is currently dead in the water?" he asked hopefully. "No secret tractor beam project you've been working on that I didn't know about?"

"No," Paterson said immediately—maybe even a little *too* immediately for Torres's liking. "Is she able to receive data?"

Torres looked up at the tactical officer who flashed a hurried thumbs-up gesture. He was being given the green light.

"Affirmative," he told Paterson.

"Good, we can remote pilot it back. Hold on a second…" The intercom clicked off and within moments the blip on the display for

117

the *Tanto* began to fly straight and true before swinging about and heading for their docking bay at a smooth pace. Torres waited in agonizing silence until the tactical officer reported that their shuttle was docked safely.

"Bring us about," he called confidently. "Return to our position in the starboard shadow of the *Venture* and prepare to target hostile ships."

The *Ichi* turned and surged away, back toward the gigantic colony ship. From this angle, it was backlit by the dull, red haze coming from the red dwarf that gave life to part of the planet.

Below them, rushing from the docking bay with all of their gear, medical personnel buzzed like highly organized flies around the repulser-powered gurneys that carried the injured or dead members of the returning team. Zero and Specter were unhurt. Miraculously Brandt and Rogers were merely shaken up after the G-forces had robbed their brains of blood flow for a few seconds too long. Marksman and cyborg were still encased in their suits which went a long way to explaining how they were unhurt, but Marcus and Chopra were banged up badly after their clash with the eight-foot-tall bugs on the surface and again in space. Byrne was also on a gurney. However, he didn't have medical personnel attending to him; his suit readouts were silent.

"Get me to the bridge," Brandt said. She stood tall, only to lose her footing almost immediately and felt her fall arrested by the painful clamp of a robotic hand around her upper body. She involuntarily hissed in pain, making Specter release his grip and use his other hand to help her back to her feet.

"Sorry," he said. "I still forget how powerful they are sometimes."

"Show off," Brandt said with a smile. "Get me to the bridge so I can report to the wheel how bad I screwed up again."

Her knees gave out a second time and she surrendered without a shred of grace to unconsciousness. Specter allowed her to fall as he changed his position, scooping her up in both arms like a child before turning and depositing her on a free gurney.

"Possible concussion through secondary blunt force trauma," he said efficiently, pressing a finger into Brandt's blue-tinged lips. "Query cyanosis and hypoxia. Loss of consciousness due to extreme G-forces experienced without protection."

The medic nodded, scanning the commander with a ruggedized datapad. She took charge of the ship's ground commander. Specter watched her go and turned to Zero and Rogers.

"Anyone volunteering to pass on that information to the captain?" he asked them.

Neither did.

Specter climbed the ladders and jogged along the decks to reach the bridge, still wearing his armor and bearing two weapons mag-locked to his thigh and back. He scanned his identity and was rewarded with the hissing sound of the bridge doors opening. He strode up to Torres's left shoulder, waiting to get his attention, but found his glowing eyes drawn to the display screen dominating the entirety of the wall ahead of them.

The screen showed the glowing blue rounds rippling out from the hull of the massive ship ahead like high-pressure water from a sprinkler system back on Earth. It seemed to Specter that every half-dozen or so gun positions concentrated their fire on an individual target that his advanced ocular implant could just about make out. Every so often a small blossom of golden sparks would explode to signify a score for their team, but he watched in horror as each sparkle of dying electricity was answered with a huge explosion and a bright pulse of blue as another ship slammed into the shields.

"Ready," Torres called, looking down at the display beside him. "And… *weapons free!*"

The hull vibrated as all of their guns opened up at once along with every warhead they had left. Specter realized that the battle he was looking at ahead of him was actually occurring behind him. They had just opened up on the leading ships not destroyed as they overshot their target and tried to loop in close to the massive hull. Warheads detonated ahead of the insectoid ships, sucking them into the collapsing space to implode them with all the might that physics had up its inescapable sleeve. Their guns thundered charged bolt after charged bolt of heavy metal. They slammed the projectiles mercilessly into the shields and hulls of the enemy and transferred their kinetic energy into devastating damage.

In an instant, through the combined might of the *Venture*'s guns and the trickery of the *Ichi*, almost two-thirds of the enemy ships had been destroyed from the first wave.

"My thanks, Captain," said a voice over the comm. Specter recognized it from a lifetime ago. "Leave the rest to us and get yourself clear. Deal with your wounded and don't stray too far."

Torres cut that comm link without responding, as he did, he spotted Specter for the first time. Specter stood slightly taller.

"Sir, Commander Brandt is in medical. Minor injuries only. We have one KIA, two badly injured and two who'll be just fine. We also still have our people on the surface—"

"I'm aware of that," Torres said irritably, pausing before he sent the man away. "Prepare all the ready troops to conduct casualty evacuations. I don't know if we're expecting boarders, but it wouldn't hurt to anticipate that."

Specter glanced at the display, too far away for any normal human to make out any detail but it may as well have been in front of him on a holo-display.

"On which ship?" he asked. This fight was clearly far from over.

~

"On my go, fire everything we have and *do not stop* until I say so or we run out of ammunition," Captain Hayes growled at his bridge crew. He seemed to enjoy the prospect of a no-holds-barred firefight when they were already half-dead in the water. As long as he had breath in his body, the *Hammer* would still be fighting.

"What do we do then, Captain?" asked his helmswoman loudly. She had a smile on her face as she nursed the battered frigate into a blockading position. Their ship would protect the huge target of the *Venture* from the twelve remaining inbound alien ships.

"*Then*, Ensign Canham, we use bad language and small arms," he replied.

"Targets marked, weapons range in one-hundred-ten seconds…" Hayes's tactical officer reported.

The captain sat down and gave his final string of orders. He expected this to be the final battle of his command. He had ordered them to come about. Some of his starboard gun positions had been damaged in their first clash. All of the ready ammunition from those damaged and useless positions was then shipped to the far side of the frigate so that the guns on that side could fire almost constantly. He planned to unload everything he had and go down shooting so that the *Venture* stood every chance of surviving the fight.

"Tactical officers: you may fire when you have a targeting solution. All gun teams: consider yourselves weapons-free when targets are in range. Concentrate fire—three guns to one target and prioritize. If you hit one, every gun will fire at its partner vessel *before* the asshole kamikazes our shields. Good huntin'. Hayes out."

"Sir, shields are down to twenty-nine percent," reported a worried voice from somewhere to his right.

"Boost all auxiliary power to shields; I want the port side running higher than everywhere else to begin with. Where are we with evacuation of the damaged decks?"

"Decks three through five all evacuated, sir," called out an officer. "Decks seven and nine still being evacuated."

"Divert all power from decks three, four and five to auxiliary banks," Hayes ordered. "Cut life support and gravity. Lock it down cold."

"Warheads away!" yelled the weapons tactical officer, nervous tension forcing the words to sound almost hysterically excited.

Hayes didn't need the words shouted to know exactly what had happened. The rippling vibrations heading from bow to stern told him that almost every warhead they had possessed was now streaking through the dark on a course to detonate, hopefully, in the path of the incoming alien ships.

They weren't the only ones to have adapted following their first clash. Before the warheads could cover the distance, the alien vessels lined up shoulder to shoulder and fired a massive salvo of shots that advanced like an orange wave of destruction. Immediately afterward, they broke away to attack from different directions in pairs.

Hayes, whichever way he looked at it, was screwed. He could move his vessel out of the way of the incoming fire. But the readout beside him confirmed that if he moved those shots would all connect with the *Venture*. The amount of fire was visible on the big display.

His ship wouldn't survive it if they took even half of the weight, but neither did he have enough time to order his crew to abandon ship. He had twenty seconds to do or at least *say* something meaningful before they were all blinked out in an instant. His only remaining option for survival was to perform another risky short jump with the Fold Drive, but that abandonment of the *Venture* was sure to spell their eventual destruction.

The *Hammer* was badly damaged and needed the help of the big colony ship to have any hope of making it out of the system in one piece.

Just as Hayes reached out for the intercom to tell his crew that they were the laziest bunch of assholes he had ever had the pleasure to fight and die alongside, another excited cry tore the still air on the bridge.

"Contact! Port side."

"The *Norton*," he said. He recognized it in a heartbeat. He couldn't believe that their sister ship had jumped in to give them a chance at life after all.

Moving slowly, the *Norton* had adjusted course after jumping in. They had seen the threat facing the beaten-up *Hammer*. Pushing every bit of power available to their port shields, the frigate's engines surged into life to slide them into position and soak up the incoming shots fired by the enemy.

Captain Hayes watched on in horror as the blinking lights of the *Norton* faltered. He stared as she began to tumble end over end as her heavy stern vertically undertook her bow. He was slammed back against his chair as a dozen shots hit their weakened shields, draining all of the reserve power he had reclaimed from the abandoned and evacuated decks in an instant. The *Norton* had saved them, but that reprieve might just have been a stay of execution.

Then he saw the attacking enemy ships on the display. They converged to finish off their weakened and injured prey that they believed were near destruction. But as Hayes continued to watch the display, those lights began to blink out in swirling, rippling vortexes.

Before she had been disabled, before she had taken the hits and been left paralyzed, the *Norton* had fired everything she had at the enemy, who were now being crushed into nothingness by the collapsing singularities devouring their would-be conquering squadron.

CHAPTER 13

Deep Space Near Proxima Centauri

Nine Hours Later

"Keep her steady," Torres warned the young man at the helm of the *Ichi*

The pilot was already being as careful as he could possibly be. The man was no Rogers, who despite being ordered to remain in medical, had tried to resume his post at the helm of the big sister of the vessel. His refusal to lie down and be examined led to him being sedated and kept in medical forcibly, which was where he remained.

"I'm trying, sir," the stand-in pilot said nervously, but he wasn't up to the task.

They had matched their speed and rate of spin to that of the tumbling frigate, the *Norton*, that still rolled end over end towards deep space. It seemed likely to do so indefinitely unless someone managed to stop them. Their power was out irretrievably. The gaping hole in their port side showed a gap right through the ship. This hole was exactly where their main power source had been before it broke free of its fixings and was sucked out into space. Now they needed a ship to dock with them externally to jumpstart them.

This meant they needed a ship large enough to stabilize the big frigate's need for power, but also one that was small enough to dock with them like a transport vessel would. The *Ichi* was the obvious choice, but without Rogers at the helm, they couldn't find a pilot with the ability to perform the stunt.

"Can't we just… wake up Lieutenant Rogers?" Sarvanto asked Torres quietly.

"The man suffered delayed-onset G-LOC; G-force-related loss of consciousness from a negative three-G spin. He's not going anywhere until his brain stops trying to swell its way out through his ears," Torres explained just as quietly.

"People," he said more loudly, "I really don't want to have to call up the admiral and explain that we can't save the ship that saved almost the entire fleet, just because we don't have a good enough driver at the wheel…"

"I'm sorry, sir," the current helmsman said in a high, wavering voice. "It's just too gosh-darned difficult to get it right."

Too gosh-darned… who the hell is this idiot? Torres thought to himself. He fought the urge to haze the kid right off his bridge and off his ship.

"Perhaps it's just a matter of co-ordination?" Paterson asked via the live comm link to his lab.

"Say what you mean, Paterson," Torres told him.

"I'm saying, Captain, that perhaps we should let someone with very good hand-eye coordination try it? Like, maybe someone with the best eyes money can buy? And hands, for that matter…"

Torres thought about it. Rogers would have another fit and probably rupture another part of his brain at hearing his natural gift of flying boiled down to simple hand-eye coordination. When he thought more, he realized that it was actually a good idea; wasn't the problem just a lack of anyone's ability to process the input fast enough to adjust the output?

"Ask him if he's up to it first," Torres said. He knew what Jake would have said but he wasn't sure what Specter would say now.

Specter, as it turned out, had retained Jake's casual ability and willingness to try anything, regardless of how dangerous it was. He had agreed instantly, walked onto the bridge and stood behind the sweating young pilot wearing a smile. The kid relinquished the controls, getting up to almost curtsy to the heavily augmented man that some people called a cyborg under their breath. He stuck around to watch as Specter dropped into his place and adjusted the seat to be best placed to activate the controls.

"Matching angle and speed of rotation," he announced in a voice that showed that he was so stone-cold that his heart only beat once a week. "Distance to docking bay eighty-nine meters... seventy...fifty... thirty... slowing approach... fifteen meters... ten..."

Torres wished he'd stop giving verbal countdowns to the collision he feared was about to happen at any moment. Just as he was forcing his eyes to stay open and not flinch from the impact, the hull reverberated with the sound of their docking clamps meeting the housing points on the bigger ship.

"Clamps engaged," the tactical officer said. "We've got them."

"Mainframe? Can you jack in to the *Norton*?" Torres asked their computer interface. He silently cursed Brandt for making him feel foolish every time he didn't have a cool name for the thing that answered him back.

"Command not recognized," the mainframe reported.

Torres sighed and gave a clear instruction using no ambiguity in his words.

"Interface complete," the dull and unobtrusive sounds of the computerized voice replied. Torres could understand why it infuriated a couple of people who felt that it sounded too calm; like it was smug and knew something the humans didn't.

"Power them up," Torres said gleefully, "and hopefully we won't have to board them."

"Command not recognized," the mainframe said again, as though being intentionally obtuse.

"Patch our power supply to the *Norton*," Torres said, not bothering to hide his annoyance at the imperceptive computer.

An acknowledging tone answered him, followed by the readout showing their available power draining by almost forty percent. The bridge lights flickered ominously, showing just how fast the depleted battery banks of the frigate were sucking their lifeblood, until the comm burst into life.

"*UNS Boken sha Ichi*, this is Captain Halstead of the *Norton*. Thanks for the bump," came the croaky Australian voice of a woman who sounded like she had been smoking the shish pipes found in the less reputable of establishments on the lunar surface.

"Captain Halstead, this is Captain Torres of the *Ichi*. Good to hear your voice. What's your situation, over?" The comm link, despite the ship's horrific damage, was crystal clear.

"We have multiple casualties on all decks… no… no idea as to the full extent of the damage… We're coming to an all-stop now, so you can disengage your dock and we should be good to dock to the *Venture*."

"Understood, *Norton*, confirm you have propulsion, life support and containment?"

A pause on the other end before she replied.

"Confirmed. Shields are holding at four percent, we have two engines on our port side still functional and life support is active in all areas where we have people left. *Norton* out."

"If that's all, Captain?" Specter asked Torres, having relinquished the helm.

"Yes. Thanks for your assistance." Specter smiled, a polite smile that didn't extend to his artificial eyes. He turned and exited the bridge, stopping as soon as the hissing sound popped closed behind him to leave him alone in the corridor leading away from the command center of the ship.

Specter reached his hand out to the wall to steady himself, feeling an unfamiliar sensation coursing through his body. His breathing, usually so slow and shallow that people were forgiven for thinking that he didn't need to suck in air, became rapid and saturated his remaining organic parts with so much oxygen that he became light-headed almost instantly. He recognized this, holding his breath to try and force the carbon dioxide levels in his body to rise and counteract the hyperventilation that was beginning to take hold of him. He staggered towards the ladder, half falling down it until he reached the level where the lab was and turned to bounce along the narrow corridors like a drunken pinball.

He reached the double doors of the lab, his breath now loud and ragged as his ocular implants began to lose focus on his surroundings. HUD information flashed up irrelevantly and the implant in his inner ear wirelessly connected at random to a ship-to-ship channel from the *Norton* without him selecting it.

"…very low power. Estimate approximately one-nine minutes to docking."

"Understood. We're coming to you."

Specter shook his head to clear the unwanted conversation from his head and severed the comm link he had accidentally hijacked. He staggered into the lab, his breathing louder and labored. He fell to his knees in the open space inside the doors as they hissed closed behind him.

"Help…" he gasped, sucking more air in and it all worse. "Some kind of… malfunction…"

Just as Doctor Paterson and two lab assistants rushed towards him, he blacked out slamming his head onto the rough metal of the deck.

"Yes, Lieutenant." Torres's voice came patiently over the poor comm line to Eze on the surface below. "I understand, but right now I literally don't have a ship to send for you. I've requested one from the *Venture*, but they are all currently engaged in rescue ops with the two damaged frigates. Wait it out."

She pursed her lips, fighting the urge to growl her frustration out. She refrained, not knowing how the nervous Kuldar skulking around in the shadows would react. She had first thought that there were only a few of them, but the translation software worked better as it learned and added to the database of sounds. She had spent her time stranded on the planet learning more about them.

"My people came here a long time ago," Asha had explained to her.

She asked if he minded her recording their conversation so that she could review it later, but she realized she had confused him by her request. Instead, she demonstrated how her suit could capture a video of him talking and played it back for him to understand. He gave his consent, speaking an excited chatter of click and croaks behind him to prompt two smaller Kuldar to come forward. They must have been Asha's children, because they sat by the sides of his chair and listened intently as he spoke.

"My people came here a long time ago," Asha said again, beginning the story of his race, "from another planet connected to the red sun."

Eze racked her brain for other red dwarf stars. Unfortunately, her knowledge of the cosmos was pretty poor.

"Our legends say of a ship that made the time and distance..." He rattled off a sound in his own tongue that didn't translate into English through Eze's earpiece. She glanced at the comm device on her forearm and saw the list of possible translations.

Irrelevant. That was the word she picked out. *So they had a Fold Drive?*

"We did this to flee our planet because the Va'alen"—Eze watched as the children flinched at the sound of the word—"destroyed our places with their machines. We took to the black beyond the sky and left our world. We came here on a very enormous ship, and our small ship came to here. We had camps on this place and started to build homes with the things we brought with us, but the Va'alen came after us and killed many. Our big ship, the one that moved through time, had to go or else be destroyed. We are all that is left of the Kuldar. Our other ship never came back, and our small ship cannot hold us all or move through time like the ship of our ancestors. We have stayed here ever since, hiding from the Va'alen."

The smaller aliens, the ones she had assumed were his children, hung their heads in sadness. Eze felt a wave of despair too, a feeling of such overwhelming melancholy and hopelessness that she had to stifle a small sob and blink away the tears she had felt prickling her eyes.

131

"So you've been stuck here, stranded without a way to get home or to another planet ever since then?" she asked.

She had to wait for the comm device to change her words into the complex kind of Morse code they understood. Asha had managed to hiss a few words in English, but that was mainly copying the simple sounds they had made. He learned fast, but not fast enough to tell the story of his people in a language he had only heard hours before.

She had asked about that, about how she felt emotions that weren't her own, about how she had known that Asha meant them no harm when they had first found him in the clearing almost half a day ago.

In answer, he smiled—his approximation of a smile that translated effortlessly between alien races with vastly different physiologies, between beings that existed trillions of light years away from each other. He lightly touched his large forehead to indicate that he could transmit emotions telepathically. Eze had understood, in a way that she couldn't comprehend or explain. She had understood that they could project their feelings and intentions, as if the Kuldar possessed some higher brain function that humans had either not yet developed or lacked the capacity to unlock.

"So... what do you want from us?" she asked tentatively.

"We are stuck on this place," Asha said passionately. "We cannot grow, and we cannot expand. We must keep away from the surface for fear of Va'alen patrols discovering our homes. They have usually left us alone since they believe we are only a few and of no consequence, but not when they have other priorities in this system."

"What priorities?" Eze asked intently. Asha smiled.

"This is something I must speak to your queen about."

"We don't have a…" Eze paused, a smile creeping up one corner of her mouth. "Asha? Did you just ask me to take you to my leader?"

CHAPTER 14

Deep Orbit of Proxima Centauri

"Ground team from *Cortez* shuttle five… Ground team, *Cortez Five*, come back, over?"

"*Cortez Five* from Viper," Eze said into her comm. "Transmitting my coordinates to you now. Be advised that the LZ has an enemy ship on the ground; do not engage it."

"Roger that, Viper. Be with you in eleven mikes. Out."

Eze smiled, looking forward to getting back to their ship and getting out of the armor. She had been in it for close to sixteen hours and felt the un-soldier-like need to step directly out of it and directly into a deep, hot bubble bath. The second colony ship, the *Cortez*, had jumped in only an hour before and had docked one of the ravaged frigates directly to its ventral bays. Desperate work was underway to repair it. The rest of the available fleet had simultaneously launched every shuttle they had with medical and damage repair teams onboard to stabilize and fix up the *Norton*. The *Cortez* had apparently been late to the party as they had suffered damage during their last jump, but they had arrived in time to help pick up the pieces, at least.

Somewhere in that confusion, a request had come through for an empty shuttle to be sent to the surface with two squads of UN troops and a mobile base station. The orders were to set up a position and guard the acquisition of an abandoned enemy spacecraft, and commander Brandt's team from the surface was to be taken directly to the *Venture* to meet with the admiral.

The contents of that shuttle, just as the alien craft on the surface, were to be treated as classified. The pilots were to stay sealed inside the cockpit. The troops sent were a double dose of CP units; all dark armor and brooding silences exuding mystery and awe.

Two suited UN personnel stepped up the ramp, the shorter one of them in armor matching the incoming troops. She paused to relay information to the new ground commander. The other was a regular UN seaman by the look of him, but the third and fourth members of the party were altogether different.

Shrouded in a long cloak with a hood that set the large head in shadow, the tall aliens stepped curiously alongside the humans. Their long legs and stooped bodies seemed so different from the humans'. Beneath those cloaks were the two Kuldar, Asha and another male called Sharga, who Asha trusted. He wore gilded armor not unlike Asha's, with an intricately chased breast plate of swirling, interlocking patterns and matching greaves that seemed more ceremonial than functional. Eze had been told that Asha was their king and Sharga their general. Both of these titles sounded impressive until she realized that the race only numbered a little over three hundred and neither of these two was actually in charge. That honor fell to Asha's mate, Nerisha, who held the royal bloodline.

Neither was armed. Eze had explained that it would be considered hostile to greet another race armed. Asha had replied without saying anything, merely projecting the *feeling* of seeing herself approaching tactically and carrying a gun.

"That was different…" she said, trailing off. She had no way to refute his answer. As weird as it felt, she was getting used to the mostly one-way telepathic communication.

Asha stayed still and resolute, slipping a small, clear mask over his face as the shuttle pressurized and made the environment slightly too oxygenated for the aliens' comfort. Sharga did the same, but he could not hide his nervousness as easily as Asha did. The shuttle took off, heading directly for the *Venture*.

Eze tried something new. She projected her thoughts to Asha, thinking of getting his attention and trying to convey that she was going to contact her immediate leader, her captain. He made no response to her mental efforts. She told him in English, hearing the translation. She felt his understanding wash over her. Bringing up a secure private channel, she boosted her signal through the shuttle's systems.

On the bridge of the *Ichi*, Torres saw the incoming channel request blinking on his terminal and recognized the CP code beside it for the encryption. She wanted to talk in private, so he asked Sarvanto to take his seat.

Stepping quickly into his cabin, he hit the blinking icon on his terminal and sat down.

"Amare," he said, using her first name warmly, "I'm glad you're safe."

"You worried about me, my little Taco?" she teased.

This earned her an annoyed look from him that quickly turned into a smile.

"I'm always worried about you," he said. "You know that."

She switched the conversation, giving her private opinion on the facts that had been relayed in her official report to the senior officers in the fleet.

"Just watch yourself around Dassiova," Torres warned her gently. "He's a hard-ass and doesn't like waiting for anything."

"Well, he's really going to enjoy having the aliens' feelings transmitted directly into his brain then," she replied sarcastically .

"Just keep it tight, okay? Did you get a look at the alien ship?" he asked.

"Yeah, just not inside. Asha said the Va'alen are sneaky assholes who like to leave booby traps."

Va'alen, Kuldar, Torres thought. *How in the hell does a classified research recon mission become a science fiction story in the space of a couple weeks?*

"Anyway, approaching the *Venture* now. Will I get to see you later?"

"I'll be there in ten minutes," he told her. "I'll need a thorough, *personal* debrief in one of the spare crew quarters as soon as I can stand both of us down for a while."

"Looking forward to it," she answered playfully. "Viper out."

"People," Dassiova said gruffly, "I'll keep this as brief as possible…"

He addressed the combined fleet captains and their flight officers in a bland and undecorated briefing room on the command deck of the fleet flagship.

"Where we expected to be doing and what we expected to *be* at this point in the mission are not as things have worked out," he said. "The *Hammer* and the *Norton* are both badly damaged, and we have no way of knowing if they can be made jump-ready in good time. We have launched deep space probes in all directions to give us advanced warning of any more alien ships incoming, but as far as we can tell, there aren't any in the immediate vicinity.

"My thanks and my condolences to Captain Hayes and Captain Halstead. The bravery and sacrifices of their crews have not gone unnoticed. You have our gratitude, for what it's worth."

Both frigate captains nodded to the admiral, both appearing as battered and bruised as their ships, but both burned with a resolve that gave the rest of them strength. The *Norton* had suffered a twenty percent loss of crew when the massive volley of fire had ventilated their ship, but now that they were docked to the top hull of the *Venture* and repairs could be affected, they were, at least for the time being, safe. Even when docked, the *Norton's* remaining guns could be brought to bear and provide a bigger defensive capability; all that was needed was an engineer capable of reprogramming the field resonance of their guns to that of the *Venture's* shielding so that the munitions could pass through and not flatten on the inside to degrade the barrier.

The *Hammer* was docked similarly to the newly arrived *Cortez*, but to her underside. The fleet of shuttles the arriving colony ship had deployed made their docking much faster than it had been possible to do with just the ships from the *Venture*.

"I know I don't need to remind anyone that what is said in this room must remain classified," he said. He eyeballed every one of them before continuing. "Captain Torres has fulfilled his recon role, albeit a little rushed. Captain?" Dassiova invited the youngest officer in the room to take the floor.

He cleared his throat and stepped forward.

"As you all know by now, my ship received contact from a sentient alien race whilst surveying the system. I sent a ground team down by shuttle, and they made face-to-face first contact. They are called the Kuldar, and they appear very different to us in their physiology. In terms of compatibility, they are accustomed to low spectrum red light and a slightly reduced oxygen content in the atmosphere. As a result of that, they have to use light breathing apparatus in our environment and vice versa."

"Tactical report?" Hayes asked, all business. He wanted to know if these new aliens were a fighting people.

"Unknown as yet," Torres answered, "but we know they have some form of stealth technology which shields their ships from visual detection. We only found them in space by their power signature. Which, incidentally, is almost the same as our own."

"How is that possible?" the flight officer from the *Norton* asked.

Torres glanced to Dassiova, who gave a short nod of permission to explain.

"Because the Kuldar had developed a faster-than-light capability years ago, and their prototype ship crash-landed on Earth. This gave us the reverse engineering of the singularity energy sources and the basic plans for the Fold Drives."

"Hold on," Captain Wright interjected. "You're telling me that in the entire universe we've somehow stumbled upon the aliens who are indirectly responsible for our recent technological leaps?"

"Yes, I am," Torres said. "But it's not quite that simple."

"You mean they have enemies, and they have just become *our* enemies," Hayes growled.

"Pretty much," Dassiova said. "We have a tactical playbook being drawn up as we speak, but these *other* aliens are very much the 'shoot first, shoot later too' types."

Torres glanced at the datapad where Eze's quick report looked back at him.

"They are called the Va'alen, and from the footage of my ground team who encountered two of them, they are a big, six-limbed predatory species with vastly overwhelming strength and resilience to our small arms."

"Did we even *try* diplomacy first?" Wright asked. He widened his eyes at Torres's expression in response.

"*We* did," he said through gritted teeth, "and *we* have two badly wounded troops, a pilot and my ground commander suffering with less severe injuries. Not to mention one man dead. Against just two of them."

"Perhaps," Wright said in a tone bordering on dangerously insolent, "a more experienced captain would have committed more resources to the team and—"

"*Perhaps*," Torres snarled back angrily, "you'd like to try taking one on yourself?"

"Alright," Dassiova said in a bored tone. "Put your dicks away before I have to get mine out and beat you both with it."

His levity succeeded in breaking the tension in the room as both Hayes and Halstead hid their sniggers. Torres and Wright backed off one another and turned to face the admiral.

"I'm told there's more to the story," he said. "If you wouldn't mind filling everyone else in before we invite our guests to join us?"

"There is," Torres said, glad for the opportunity to step down from an unnecessary confrontation. "The Kuldar fled their home world in another system using their jump drive capability after the Va'alen appeared in their own system and began strip-mining their planet. The Va'alen couldn't be reasoned with; they just killed them.

The survivors took off and settled on Proxima Centauri b which has the same kind of environment as their original planet."

"Orbiting a red dwarf?" Halstead asked, frowning so her eyebrows almost met in the middle of her forehead.

"Yes, it seems like their goldilocks band is a little different to ours and they thrive in a temperate low spectrum light environment," Torres explained.

She shrugged as he continued.

"The Va'alen found them there, and the ship with the Fold Drive jumped away and, as we know, eventually crash-landed on Earth. The survivors left behind on Proxima b had to hide out as the Va'alen patrolled the system to build something. It's not clear what they're here for, but it seems to be a very remote outpost."

"And where do we stand in the middle of this?" Wright asked Dassiova directly.

"We're about to find out," he said as he dimmed the lights in the room.

He turned and nodded to the CP soldier guarding the door. The armored man stepped outside, returning with Eze who still wore her armor but had removed the helmet. Behind her were two tall, greenish gray-skinned humanoids with thin limbs and huge skulls.

They wore hooded robes over metallic armor plates, which seemed more decorative than functional; parts of their leathery skin were exposed. They touched their long, three-fingered hands together in a gesture of supplication or respect, then both in turn touched the thumb and forefingers of their right hands to their large foreheads. Almost everyone in the room forced down the urges to stare open-mouthed and to return the gesture. Every one of them was overwhelmed by a feeling of trepidation and nervous excitement. None of them knew where these feelings came from, and each was left unable to speak for a few seconds. The translator on Eze's arm module was removed and placed on the table with the volume up.

The lead alien spoke in a croaking rattle.

"Esteemed King of the human peoples," the translator said. The computerized voice coming out of it made a few people snap their mouths shut to avoid a laugh escaping. "I am Asha, King of Kuldar and servant to Her Majesty, Queen Nerisha. This is our chief warrior, Sharga. We thank you for your visiting here."

"Err, you're welcome," Dassiova said, thrown by being addressed as royalty. "I am *Admiral* Elias Dassiova; commander of the Ninth Earth Fleet and Captain of this ship, the *Venture*."

Asha touched his thumb and forefinger to his forehead again in greeting, which Dassiova found himself mimicking. This made him feel foolish. He introduced the other captains in turn, giving their names and ships as each of them returned the curious gesture as their admiral had done.

"King Asha," Dassiova said respectfully, "can you tell us more about the Va'alen and why they are here in this system?"

"You have learned of how they forced us from our first home?" he asked hopefully as he looked at Eze.

"We have," Dassiova said. "Tell us more about them."

"They want only death and war," Kuldar said sadly. His telepathic abilities made everyone in the room feel an unexpected wave of hopelessness. "We try for many lifetimes to make a peace with them, but never they stop killing. We hide. We cannot go other places."

"So you don't have the capability to travel at faster-than-light speeds any longer?" asked Dassiova.

"No. This one ship have that engine and gone few lifetimes ago. Leave only shuttle which we try no use as Va'alen patrol."

"And why are the Va'alen patrolling here? What are they doing? Do they have a home world in this system? Do they have FTL capabilities?"

Asha almost took a step backwards under the onslaught of the questions from the captain of the *Cortez*. He radiated a hint of panic, which was gone as soon as it was felt.

"Va'alen come to take minerals and ores from worlds to take back home. They live in their ships and come through the gateways."

"So they're here mining resources and travel between systems through a... *gateway?* A portal device?"

"Yes, the ring in space that bring their ships." Asha drew back his cloak and the room seemed to stiffen fearing a weapon. Instead he laid out a flat stone, which flickered to life and gave a red holographic display projected above it.

"Va'alen gateway," Asha said, showing them the image of a massive circular device in space with another large ball of an object.

He zoomed in with his fingertips, showing them how the smaller Va'alen ships, like the ones who had swarmed the fleet, attached to the ball like they were docking to a central hive.

"Gateway leads to another system of stars. No gateway, no Va'alen here."

"There's the simple solution, sir," Hayes said confidently. "We smash their portal and destroy the remaining ships in this sector. Then they can't come after us. The resources are ours, along with the habitable planets."

"How very simplistic of you," Wright said, disdainfully. "Do you recall two warships being torn apart recently?"

"I do, Wright," Hayes said dangerously. "Care to enlighten me as to *your* experience of being on the receiving end of their weapons and suicide bombing runs?"

"Enough," Dassiova said quietly, silencing them both. "Please accept my apologies," Dassiova said formally to Asha. "We have suffered a great loss of our people fighting the Va'alen today."

"I understand *Ad-mih-rahl*," Asha said, sounding out the word in syllables instead of letting the unfamiliar word be mistranslated. "We have suffered by them for generations, so we know your pain in this thing."

Dassiova nodded and performed a kind of bow. He was overcome by the solemn nature of their words and the emotions he wasn't expecting to experience.

"In this we can help you," Asha said. "As we saw, your weapons are not good against the Va'alen, but we can show you how to make Va'alen weapon."

The implications of his words were huge. The promise of such devastatingly superior weaponry could make an enormous difference on Earth, but the overall promise to meld alien technology with their own opened up astounding new horizons to them. Dassiova considered it, knowing that the decision was above his paygrade and had to be reported to his masters on Earth. But he also knew that those in power would always seek to obtain and control any weapon they didn't already possess. It was a catch twenty-two; was he doing the right thing for the wrong reason, or the wrong thing for the *right* reason?

"Our shields," he said as he pressed his advantage, "are vastly superior in our system, yet here they barely worked against those ships…"

"This we cannot make change," Asha said regretfully, bowing his large head and genuflecting as he had before in apology.

"So where is this ring and their… their *hub*?" Torres asked.

"They are on the other side of the brighter sun of the two," Asha said.

"Alpha Centauri?" Hayes asked.

Nods all round confirmed that Alpha *was* the brighter of the twin suns in the nearby system.

"That's what? Over a light year from here? Two?" Halstead asked. "Sir, we are down one main power source, have expended over half our munitions and are in generally pretty bad shape. We cannot be considering this."

"Duly noted, Captain," Dassiova said carefully.

"But, sir," she said again as she took a half step forward. She froze as Dassiova fixed her with a cold look.

"I said, Captain, that your objection was noted." Halstead retraced her half step and said nothing more. "King Asha," the admiral asked, "what will this assistance costs us?" Asha waited for the translation, looking at Eze as though she could help him understand better.

"What do you want from us?" she asked him.

Asha smiled awkwardly, showing small and pointed teeth that did nothing to support the intended gesture of reassurance. "We wish to claim asylum from humans of Earth."

CHAPTER 15

Bōken Sha Ichi

Jake woke up, sucking in a big gasp of air as though he had passed out when drowning. Lab assistants rushed to him. They immediately began tapping at screens and staring intently at displays, but none of them spoke to him. None of them reassured him that he was going to be fine. Nobody told him it was okay.

His hands flapped at his body as he sat up, checking himself over to see that he was still there and that his legs had not been blown off like in his nightmare.

It had felt so real; all the fear and the searing pain as he ran away from the bomb. The rush of force and the heat enveloping him.

Then blackness. Then nothing.

As his hands gripped onto his legs, the appendages felt strange to him. His grip was painfully strong, but the sensation he experienced wasn't pain. It was more like the imagination of pain without the receptors activating properly. He flinched, feeling that his legs were hard and angular beneath the rubberized pants he wore. When he looked at his hands he saw that they were robotic. He focused on those hands as he held them before his face, and when he concentrated on them his vision zoomed in like a riflescope and showed him the minute detail of the textured fingertips.

He completely lost it.

Roaring in fear and confusion, Jake threw his arms out wildly to clear a path through the people and get off the bed. When he connected with one, he launched the young man in white scrubs halfway across the room, watching him slide the rest of the way on his back.

Jake stood, aiming to jump over the heads of the many people preventing his escape. Instead of dropping down on the other side of them, he sailed through the air like he wore a jet pack and landed a full fifteen feet away from the bed with perfect balance.

"Whoa there, calm it down, man…" a familiar yet confusingly distant voice said, trying to soothe him.

Jake turned and saw the young man he had joined the UNPF with, who he had trained and lived with for years, and with whom he had fought alongside until…

Only it wasn't the same man. This was an older version of him, wearing a white lab coat instead of the uniform or armor that they lived in. He had grown a goatee, which made him look older still, and the lines around his eyes were deeper and more pronounced than they had been before.

"Jamie…?" Jake asked, uncertainly.

"Calm down, Specter," Paterson said. He inched toward him with both hands up as though worried he would attack at any point.

"Specter?" Jake asked, confused even more. He half recognized the person in front of him it sounded like the man thought he was someone else. "Why are you calling me that? What the hell is going on here?"

"You've had a… a *relapse*," Jamie Paterson told him, "and a head injury. You need to sit down before you hurt yourself or someone else."

That made sense to Jake. The last thing to go through his head before he blacked out was the enormous blast.

In actual fact, the last thing to have gone through his head had been a piece of steel casing from the bomb, but Paterson didn't think that was the best piece of information to lead with at this time.

"Tell me your name," he said as he approached cautiously. "My *name*? The hell are you talking about, dumbass?" "Humor me, buddy," Paterson said.

"It's me," he said with an annoyed huff. "Jake. You know? The guy you signed up with? The one who's been carrying you for almost five years?"

"I've been carrying you, more like," Paterson said with a smirk. "Just do me a favor and let me give you this, okay?" He produced a hypodermic infuser. "Just something to slow your heart rate, that's all."

"I… I dunno…" Jake said as he took another pace backwards and saw everyone in the lab flinch in fright at his movement.

"It's okay, Jake, just relax," Paterson said, pressing the button on the small device. He administered the strong sedative to the exposed skin of Specter's neck.

Jake dropped, clanging to the floor like the mostly metal cyborg that he was and making a loud noise ring out. Paterson stood to his full height, much taller than most men, and dropped the nicey-nicey approach. Instead, he found himself a pissed off scientist wondering why he'd just had to deactivate someone else's dangerous pet science project. His anger and frustration went deeper than that, he knew, because he'd just had the briefest of conversations with a man he had come to terms with after having lost him years before.

"Get that man medical attention," he ordered. He pointed at the groaning, writhing lab tech who had been thrown bodily through the air. "And for God's sake, get those Hyper guys down here to check on what's happened inside his head."

Brandt had been allowed out of medical with the strict instructions that she was not to be on her feet for more than half an hour at the most. Moreover, she was not, under any circumstances, to operate machinery or weaponry for another twenty-four hours. She had readily agreed to the medical officer's terms, just as she would have agreed to fetch unicorn blood, simply to get the hell out of there. She had walked slowly to the bridge where she entered to find one of the senior tactical officers sitting in the big chair. All eyes turned to regard her, and since she didn't appear to be injured, the chair was vacated for her. She waved the officer back down and sat carefully in her usual seat, where she leaned back to rest her stiff neck.

"They tell me the pain and stiffness'll be worse tomorrow," she complained in a loud whisper. "Like it can get any goddamned worse…"

"Captain on deck," cried out a young and eager voice, earning himself quiet admonishments from those nearby.

Torres was one of the ship's captains who insisted that the old rules were no longer relevant in some ways. Being heralded as some kind of deity everywhere he walked onboard the ship was tiresome, and he had insisted that his crew go about their tasks without commenting on his presence unless he specifically instructed them to do otherwise.

Dassiova had done the same, but on his ship with over six thousand people afloat with him, he found that he couldn't even make it to the head with being saluted fifty times.

Brandt turned as Torres and Eze returned, and looked with one eye closed to help her focus. Torres looked at his battered commander, deciding whether to send her away or tell her the news that he couldn't wait to share.

"Briefing room," he told her quietly, "then you're going back to medical."

"You'll have to shoot me to keep me there," she warned him groggily, waving an admonishing finger.

Torres ignored her remark; she would understand that her suggestion was being taken under advisement. The door to the briefing room hissed close behind them and Torres remained standing as the two women sat.

"Want the big news?" he asked Brandt.

"Hit me," she slurred with one eye closed. Torres hesitated, not sure if she would even remember what he was about to tell her. His need to go over the facts so that they would solidify in his mind pressed him forward.

"So, the Kuldar aren't from this system but from another red dwarf in another system light years away. They've been stranded here since some of them escaped their planet fleeing the Va'alen. They—"

"I had the history lesson on the planet's surface," she said, interrupting him. "Can we skip to the point, Captain?"

"The Kuldar want asylum," he said, his excitement not dulled by her response, "and in return for helping them, we will get access to stealth and weapons technology beyond anything we can imagine."

"But we just got new guns…" Brandt muttered.

Torres looked at Eze who seemed to intuit his meaning in an instant.

"Okay, Commander," she said as she forcibly helped the groggy woman up from her chair. "Time for you to rest now."

She helped her from the room, leaving the bridge and climbing carefully down the ladder to the quarters they shared. Eze put Brandt in her bed, pulling off her boots and tucking the covers under her arms like a child. She slipped from the room to shed her armor in the nearest charging station before walking quickly back to the room.

She stank. Her hair was matted and greasy, her clothes felt stiff where they had been pressed against her body inside the confines of her suit, and her skin had a film on it that she needed to scrub away. She slipped back into their quarters, checked that the dazed commander was still sleeping off the effects of the medication and the mild concussion, and stepped out of her clothes and into a shower. Eze enjoyed a long soak that eased the tension in her cramped muscles, cranking up the temperature bit by bit until the heat was too intense. She killed the flow of water, standing inside the cubicle as she worked the tiny amount of liquid soap up into a lather than covered her entire hair and body. Then she switched the shower back again on to let it wash away all of the sweat and the stress that went with it.

She dried herself with a small towel, removing the water from her small but athletic frame, and dressed in new underwear and a new flight suit. She pulled the suit from the thin cellophane packaging, which she screwed into a ball and threw into the recycling chute. She stepped out of the small bathroom cubicle, saw that Brandt had rolled over onto her face and was snoring softly, and slipped her feet into her boots. Eze picked up her comm device and crept from the cabin in silence.

She stepped lightly down the corridors of the crew quarters, checking her device for the right cabin designation. Once she found it, Eze looked left and right for anyone watching before scanning her implant and entering as soon as the door opened. Immediately, strong hands grabbed her upper arms and gripped her tightly. She didn't struggle against them, just let herself be pulled into him and felt lips press hard into her own. She relented, relaxing into the embrace, and wrapped her arms up and around the taller person waiting in the room for her.

"I don't have long," Torres whispered in between kissing her.

"I know," she responded. "So stop wasting time by talking…"

Two thousand kilometers away, Admiral Dassiova sat pensively behind the desk in his private quarters. Outside the chambers he knew there was a world of activity running twenty-four-seven, especially with the damaged *Norton* docked to his ship's spine. The ship had an army of shuttles and crewmembers in EVA suits swarming over it to repair the worst of the damage. Dassiova knew that inside the *Norton* they were preparing to connect one of the many power generator units, one of the big singularity drives, from his own intentionally over-powered ship. This drive would run the smaller frigate until more permanent repairs could be made. He knew that the massive inter-ship repair and relief efforts were in hand, and that he didn't need to concern himself with the minutia of the daily operations any longer; he was forced to be a big picture guy now.

Having spent so many years with his hands on the reins—as a CP special operator, a team leader and as a unit commander—he was still unaccustomed to allowing all of those important jobs to be taken care of by other officers. He knew they were competent, knew they were capable and trustworthy and knew that they would get the job done. They should only bother him if there was a matter he needed to know about and make a judgment on; or if something needed the ratification of the admiral. In those few and far between instances, he would find himself presented with problem and solutions in one briefing. It was a strange feeling, sitting back and having the world revolve around him, leaving him to make decisions about overall policy and not the fine details of things.

He said that the crews of the *Venture* and the *Cortez* should offer all aid available to repair the frigates, and it was done. He didn't need to know, or even *get* to know, about the specific problems and the top triage list of repairs. There was a whole level of management introduced between him and those facts.

It was impossible to know those facts; not with superficial damage to the *Venture,* along with two-dozen systems that had malfunctioned during their first combat test. The damage to their pair of frigates was close to catastrophic, and without the two colony ships, then the frigates would likely be doomed. As it was, they could remain firmly docked and suckle at the teat until they made it back home, and he hadn't even had chance to read the full report of the *Ichi.* Though he had skimmed enough to read the parts about the aliens.

The aliens, he thought to himself. *Goddamned* aliens! *Last month I was still trying to get used to being called admiral and worrying about having so many people under my command and now… now I've led those people into the middle of an alien war that's been going on for hundreds of years. Have I brought Earth into that war now, too?*

The dull chatter of an incoming call on the subspace array interrupted his spiraling cycle of depressing thoughts. He sat up, smoothed his uniform coat and set his jaw tightly before hitting the icon to accept it. Facing him on the screen was another admiral and a UNID agent conspicuously uniformed in her plain suit. Another man was there, also suited but giving the impression that his public and winning smile appearance mattered more than the words he said; there was something behind his eyes that was altogether too calculating. Too false.

Politician, Dassiova's brain yelled at him in warning. "Admiral," the other admiral said awkwardly.

"What's the situation?" the UNID representative asked brusquely. She didn't seem hostile, just without any natural ability to conduct small talk.

"You have the report?" Dassiova asked. He didn't want to have to go over his battle losses again.

"We do," she answered, "but briefly in your own words if you would?"

Dassiova sighed, but recovered himself. "After your communiqué to support the *Ichi* in this system, I jumped the *Venture* and the *Hammer* in. We were immediately faced with incoming hostile alien ships fighting in a configuration we did not recognize.

"They possess superior weapons capabilities as well as a kind of distortion field that shrouds them from targeting systems; we adapted to that and have developed algorithms to predict their movements in combat. Concentration of fire on possible trajectories allowed us limited success in battle."

"We have the contact report, Admiral," his ranking peer said gently. "I think these people want to know more about the other races and the, err, *situation* there…"

"The situation is simple; they are survivors of a genocide here that are seeking our asylum. In return, they're offering advanced technologies, which we know have merit. Our own FTL capability is based on their very *old* technology."

"And what of their enemies there?"

"They're called the Va'alen," he said, rolling his tongue around the unfamiliar word. "I presume you've seen the footage from the ground team?" They nodded, so he continued.

"We are in the process of recovering one of their ships left behind on the surface, and we have a physical sample of their physiology. Hopefully that will yield a lot of actionable intel on how to defeat them if we face another battle."

The other suit cleared his throat, sitting forward for the first time to speak. "Admiral? What are your thoughts on what we should do? Is this technology worth potentially starting an inter-system war with another race? Especially with one so... *war-like?*"

"Like we aren't, sir?" he asked.

His words made the other man's winning smile fade into a flash of anger, replaced in an instant with the concerned look of a man addressing the concerns of his constituents.

"I mean, Admiral, is this a fight we can win?"

And there it is, Dassiova thought, *the bottom line. They haven't asked about the probe reports from the other planets because they've already seen the data and decided that this system could be mined for resources; otherwise there wouldn't be a conversation to be had. I'm being asked to sign off on whether we can beat the natives.*

He sat forward, interlocking his fingers and looking hard at the three faces looking back at him.

"I need a fleet three times this size," he began, aiming high with the hopes of getting even a third of what he asked for. "I need three FTL-capable carrier support ships with a half-dozen frigates attached to each one. I need all of those ships to be running a shield battery at least three hundred percent above what we *thought* was the maximum requirement, and I need a mobile forge ship."

"Anything else, Admiral?" the UNID woman asked. She fixed him a look with one eyebrow raised as though he had just asked for the blood of their firstborn children to be served alongside a gallon of peanut M&Ms with all the yellow and brown ones picked out.

"Yes," he said, leaning back. "If we somehow *take* this system, then we need to *keep* it. We will need a station here, permanent planetary bases if the other planets are suitable, and we need a defense grid. Now this goes well beyond my paygrade, but I don't think our territory can do this all by itself."

CHAPTER 16

Proxima Centauri B

The team of engineers stood with their hands on their hips looking up at the looming hulk of the alien ship. It seemed to be staring back at them with motionless malevolence, almost daring them to try and climb inside it to unlock its secrets. The scaffolding that they had erected and draped over it looked ridiculous, as though someone had balanced matchsticks on top of a dead dragonfly.

"Well, I'm officially stumped," one of them said.

He pulled away his breathing mask to stick a finger in his right nostril to perform a casual excavation. The female specialist beside him let out a sigh at being surrounded by animals, but she had to admit that she was out of ideas also.

"Hey, aren't we supposed to be getting help from the little green men?"

"Don't call them that, Hooper," she said in a hushed growl as she cast a look around to see if anyone else had heard him.

They had yet to see one of the creatures that lived on this planet, but she had a constant feeling that she was being watched with fascination. Another scan of the dark tree line showed nothing visible to her naked eye.

"Relax, Brooks," he said. "They are little and green, aren't they? And I assume that some of them *must* be men, otherwise how do they get little green kids?" He waggled his eyebrows at her in a way that he thought was seductive, though she found it repulsive.

"You're an asshole, Hooper," she said, turning away in further disgust as he inspected the yield on the end of his finger and cleaned it off in his mouth.

"Yeah, well, asshole or not, I'm going in. Hold my metaphorical beer," he said.

He grabbed the extendable ladders and placed them against the black, reflective surface of the cockpit to climb up. He tried prying it open, getting nowhere. Brooks rolled her eyes—why did he think something that could withstand the pressure of space would give up just because he waved a crowbar at it?

Then he slid the tool back into his utility belt, took out a battery-operated disc cutter and spun it up.

"Hooper, the hell are you doing?" Brooks asked from below the ladder. "You know we were ordered not to damage…" She trailed off as a wave of fear, of sudden panic enveloped her. It almost crushed her, threatening to take her legs out from beneath her as the fear rose into something bordering on desperation. She had no idea why, but she *knew* that something bad was about to happen.

"Hooper, no! Stop!" she yelled.

"Almost there, darlin'," Hooper called back, ignoring her command completely.

Brooks looked about wildly, seeing others nearby, distressed just as she was. She made a decision—she shouted at everyone to get away from the ship and run, to get to the trees away from the screeching noise of metal being sliced open. Her own feet propelled her, moved faster by a compulsion to get away. When she looked up to see where she was running, her breath caught in her throat.

She was looking at the distant form of two gray-skinned humanoids with large heads and thin limbs beckoning her desperately toward them.

She didn't reach the aliens in time. The explosion of the alien ship burst out laterally, throwing her toward the creatures, then suspending her in midair as her ears were deafened and rang. Her body hung as if frozen in between gravity and weightlessness. She felt forces pull on her, dragging her back towards the exploding ship as the thin fingers of her would-be rescuer reached out for her desperately. Their eyes met her own, light hazel appearing as black as the big, dark elliptical ones of the aliens. The creatures radiated panic and fear for her. She touched their skin, feeling the rough dimples brush against her own soft hands as she was pulled back towards the tiny collapsing singularity where the ship had been a second before. Her scream was cut off after a split second. She was crushed into nothingness.

"Report, Mister Sarvanto," Torres barked as he walked onto the bridge only minutes before his day shift was rostered to begin.

"We have detected an explosion on the surface of Proxima Centauri b, sir. It has a singularity field indictor on the data, but it's not anything of ours."

"Hail the engineering team on the surface."

"Tried that, sir," the comm officer shot back. "No response to hails."

"Keep trying," he told her before turning back to Sarvanto who was manning the tactical station. "Can you get me eyes on?"

"On that now, Captain…"

He glanced up at the main viewscreen as the orbital image zoomed in over such a massive distance that it seemed to Torres that he was actually falling towards the black planet bathed in low, red light.

"Enhance that, if you can," he ordered.

The image brightened as though someone had cranked up the contrast. The landing zone where the engineering team from the *Venture* had gone under their protection, the one where the abandoned Va'alen ship had been left ready to be picked apart and studied, was gone.

Not *gone* gone, more of the huge-crater-slash-no-longer-in-existence kind of gone.

"What the hell…?" muttered the comm officer. She looked up from her terminal to gawp open-mouthed at the bomb site far below.

Torres turned to Sarvanto and gave him quiet orders. "Dispatch a team. I know the *Tanto* isn't fully operational, but she can fly; get some medics and a team down there RFN."

Sarvanto nodded his assent and turned away to make it happen.

"Aren't you supposed to be on the radio, Petty Officer?" Torres asked the comm officer.

"But… there's nobody there to—"

"Hail the *Venture*," he told her quickly. She snapped out of her daze and tapped at her terminal. "Channel open."

"*UNS Venture*, this is the *Boken sha Ichi* Actual, over."

"*Ichi* Actual, *Venture*, five-by-five, send over."

"*Venture*, are you reading what just happened on the surface with your team? Did you receive any comm traffic prior to the explosion?"

"That's a negative, Captain. We read the same sensor spike but had no traffic prior… wait one… compliments of the admiral,

Captain Torres, he requests you send a team as first responders as you are the closest."

"Already dispatched, *Venture*. *Ichi* out."

"Sir," Sarvanto said as he put his small headset down. He had vacated tactical for another member of the bridge crew to run in his place. "Zero has three troops and a medical team of six are mustering now. Launching in four minutes."

Torres said nothing and simply nodded once. Telling Sarvanto that four minutes was three and half too long would serve only to betray how nervous and helpless he felt, sitting in the big chair instead of running around going bang-bang with a gun. No matter how good he felt doing that, it was hardly a big picture role. No, he had to sit back and trust his people to do their jobs as well as he had always done his own.

Zero ordered the pilot to hover two hundred meters above the LZ and scan the surface. The immediate readings showed trace radiation from a singularity collapse roughly half the size of one of their ship's warheads. In itself, that was a devastating enough explosion, but luckily the radiation wouldn't affect the emergency relief team, as long as they stayed inside their suits.

"Any life signs?" he asked the co-pilot who was running the sensor sweep.

"I'm reading a dozen, maybe more, of the aliens about three klicks out," she reported, "but nothing in the LZ."

"Any sign of the enemy ship or the shuttle from the *Venture*?"

"Negative, sir."

"I'm not a sir," he told her. "I'm Zero, or a buddy or a dude. In some circumstances I'm a, 'hey, asshole,' but I'm never a sir."

"Sure thing, dude," she responded. She was unsure as she always was with men like Zero, the elusive and usually arrogant CP types with their cool little callsigns and their shield logo stamped on their armor. She had learned they did this so you never knew *who* they were, only *what* they were. This guy seemed different though, she thought. Less of an asshole at any rate. So far, at least.

Zero paused, looking at the radiation readings. He peered at them, judging whether it was worth the hassle. He would have to decontaminate himself and the entire shuttle just to walk around a crater where he knew nothing remained that he had any interest in.

"Take us to a safe distance north," he instructed. "I need to trade some light beer and blue jeans…"

"What does *that* mean?" the pilot asked as he banked the ship to comply.

"It means I need to talk to the natives," Zero said absently. "Jeez, read a data file…"

Zero had the shuttle put down in a small clearing about four clicks northeast.

It was way beyond the safe minimum distance from the radiation, and it was also the only place that the pilot could get the *Tanto* to fit with the hasty repairs she had undergone. She wasn't in the best shape after being battered and disabled in space only hours before.

It wasn't just the *Tanto* that was in need of repairs: Zero's commander was beat up herself and her armor was toast.

Still, Zero reminded himself, *could always be worse…*

"Report a total loss to Captain Torres and dust off out of sight," Zero said as he hit the rear ramp release. "I'll holler when I need a ride."

The ship hovered mere inches from the soft, spongy moist ground just long enough for Zero to step down and crouch to save the thrusters from heating him too much inside his tin can. He stood, watching as the small ship went up out of sight. He walked for a while, finding a raised tree root that was so black it seemed to shimmer purple.

He rested his rifle against the tree and sat down on the fat root, leaned back under the wide, rubbery leaves and waited.

Zero tested his own theory, waiting until he began to feel a tickle of emotion that didn't originate with him. He was rewarded with a sensation that transported him back to his childhood when he played hide and seek with his older sister. She always lost, mostly because she couldn't stop herself from giggling when she knew he was near and even at that young age, he was a stone-cold operator and never failed to capitalize on a mistake his enemy made.

"It's okay," he said into the comm device attached to his left fore-arm. He waited for it to translate into the croaks and clicks of Kuldari.

"I need to talk to one of you," he said, taking a gamble on his next words given the feelings they radiated. "To one of your adults."

After a pause, a high-pitched series of rattling clicks sounded, coming back through his translation software.

"You come with us?"

It had to be a kid, he knew that somehow from the feelings he felt when they were near. There seemed to be more than one, he knew, as the bushes ahead of him in the low light moved. Two pairs of dark eyes blinked at him. Zero stood slowly, picking up his rifle carefully by the barrel and mag-locking it to his back.

"Let's go," he said, seeing their feet move excitedly as the translation reached them.

They set off through the dense foliage and boggy terrain, forcing Zero to keep up a fast pace which he knew he couldn't have maintained without a powered armor suit. The journey was short but intense, and the path twisted and turned as chaotically as the minds of the children who devised the route. Arriving at the main underground complex of round chambers where the others had met with Asha, he was stopped. Standing before him were two large adults bearing short staffs and wearing curious armor that seemed decorative. It comprised only simple leg and forearm greaves and a small breastplate.

"Stop! You are not permitted to be here in this place," his comm device translated for him robotically.

"I apologize," Zero said, stepping back and bowing his head to touch the fingertips of his right gauntlet to the forehead of his helmet. His detailed research of the reports had been thorough in anticipation of such an opportunity. "I wish to speak with someone about the explosion." He kept his head bowed but looked up at the two warriors through his visor. "With your permission?" He held his hands by his helmet. A clicking noise translated into text on his comm device as [GRUNT?].

He deactivated the helmet function on his HUD, ensuring that he programmed an oxygen release to allow him to show his face for a limited time. The pair of Kuldar blocking his path couldn't hide their reactions; a flash of fear followed by curiosity and disbelief. Why he inspired fear in the tall, large-headed aliens Zero had no idea, but the feeling they projected, as fleeting as it had been, was unmistakable.

"Is there someone who will speak to me?" he asked again, standing to his full height as they gestured him inside.

"*Tanto* to Zero, receiving you five-five. We have your transponder and will be with you in… three mikes."

"Acknowledged," Zero said, his jaw set tightly underneath the helmet.

He waited in a different clearing large enough to accommodate their small ship. Hearing the accounts of how the ship had exploded when they had tried to open it, of how the engineering team had been blown out, then sucked back in and crushed into nothing, had angered him. At the engineers' stupidity but also at the wasteful loss of life. What had angered him more, what made his need to get back to orbit in a hurry, was the rest of the story that their new friends hadn't told them before.

And that vital piece of intelligence made every second they stayed in that system potentially fatal.

CHAPTER 17

Proxima Centauri B Orbit

"No, sir," Torres said stiffly to the admiral. They again spoke via secure comm link from their respective private quarters. "What I'm saying is that the Kuldar appear not to have been entirely truthful about the Va'alen presence in this system."

"And this intel came directly from other Kuldar on the surface, correct? Who authorized another contact mission, anyway?"

"Indirectly, Admiral, you did," Torres answered carefully. He hastily continued before the famous Dassiova stare had a chance to take hold of his soul and crush it like a canary held too tightly. "You requested a response team investigate the sensor spike at the LZ."

"I requested first responders, Captain. I did not specify that your mavericks invite themselves over for alien supper."

"Understood, sir, and full responsibility lies with me," Torres lied smoothly. "I briefed my team leader to find out what happened, and in the process of finding that out he spoke with the Kuldar on the surface. They, without solicitation, informed him of the updated Va'alen threat."

Dassiova narrowed his eyes momentarily, knowing that he was being bullshitted. He couldn't help but appreciate the deft way that it was being handled. He let out a growl, which he quickly controlled into a throat-clearing cough as he shifted position in his seat.

"And how reliable is this new intel?" Dassiova asked.

166

"I'd argue it's as reliable as the intel we have from the ones already onboard, sir. It's from an untested source, can't be corroborated or refuted at this time and isn't verified by any of our assets."

"Yes, yes, Captain," Dassiova said with obvious annoyance. "Quote any more protocol at me and I'm likely to remember that you're not even supposed to be in charge of that ship... ah, *shit*..." The admiral stood up and began pacing. "I clearly can't ignore what your man has reported, so I guess we need another talk with our new friends. That is, unless you feel like jumping to where this place is supposed to be and corroborating the intel yourself?"

"Sir, I have no doubts as to the capabilities and bravery of my crew, but if the enemy *are* there and we *are* detected, we would be bringing down a metric shit-ton of enemy—in force and with superior firepower—onto a damaged fleet."

Dassiova said nothing, musing over the dilemma he faced. He could return home and report that they'd had their asses handed to them by what was effectively a race of eight-foot-tall cockroaches. Add to that defeat a cargo hold full of other aliens who originally possessed the technology that gave his fleet the ability to reach the new system, and he could forget staying an admiral. That new system was where they had thought the technology had originated, when in fact, the Centauri system had been a kind of no-man's-land where none of the indigenous life had evolved sufficiently to travel into space.

Proxima b provided a unique set of circumstances that allowed life to emerge, and one where the Kuldar could easily survive.

What the Kuldar hadn't told them, and what they hadn't progressed far enough into the system to discover for themselves, was that a planet existed in almost the same cosmic conditions as Earth, providing what could potentially be a mirror planet of their own overcrowded home world.

The ramifications of that discovery, if it proved to be true, were unfathomable. It would mean no more covering under domes on the surface of a cold, barren rock or, worse still, living in brutal conditions on Mars. Humans could be done living under the same domes on a planet that constantly shook and threatened to kill them every day.

No, he told himself, *this could be the real thing. A second Earth. Earth mkII. That would be one hell of a piece of news to bring home, and if I had proof of its existence, then the whole of humanity would combine and forget their petty squabbles to build a fleet unparalleled in human history.*

Hundreds of ships, from all the four territories of Earth, all with the advanced weaponry that my fleet managed to secure, and all for the price of rehoming a few hundred aliens and giving them a ship with a Fold Drive.

"I understand, Captain," he said, "and I do not suggest a suicide mission under any guise. Let me formulate an approach and I'll let you know. Keep this between us for now. Dassiova out."

The screen went black, leaving Torres alone in the near darkness inside his quarters. He decided that he wouldn't wait for the facts to be relayed to Earth, only for the politicians and the shareholders and the spooks and their lawyers to pore over it with their personal agendas firmly in mind. Instead, he went to seek the truth from their guests.

He walked out, striding along the corridor and almost colliding with Brandt coming up a ladder.

"Going somewhere, Captain?" she asked, restored to her former self.

"Clearly," he responded witheringly. This prompted a stunned look of surprise on her face. He stopped, let out a sigh and hung his head with his back still to her.

"On me, Commander," he said in a tired, apologetic tone.

Brandt fell in just behind his right shoulder to match his pace if not his intensity.

"You armed?" he asked.

"Always," she answered, smirking.

"Good, because in a minute I might need you to put a gun to an alien's head and get us the truth. You down with that?" Brandt hesitated a heartbeat, which for her was half a heartbeat too long.

"Whatever you need."

The mostly empty cargo bay, converted in a hurry to accommodate the few Kuldar already onboard and in anticipation of almost four hundred more, was bathed in a warm red light from the hastily recommissioned UV lamps.

Torres and Brandt entered, passing the two armored sentries guarding the door, and looked around for Asha.

Torres pursed his lips, as he did when he was about to say something he shouldn't. He caught Brandt's eye in the gloomy interior of the big area. Brandt stifled her own facial contortion and looked away in case a simple twitch of his mouth prompted her to laugh. Torres whispered it anyway: a weak joke that was beneath his station.

"They all look the same..."

Brandt coughed loudly to cover her response to the jest that nobody should've found funny. It served the purpose. One of the aliens stepped forward with an entourage of two and greeted them with the touch of his forehead that was becoming familiar to them.

'Comm-an-durr Brrandt," Asha said in his loud whisper. "And Cap-tenn Tore-ezz." As he finished, he bowed his head and touched the fingers to his forehead again.

Both Brandt and Torres experienced a hint of sinful pride coming from him as he demonstrated his grasp of English. Their comm devices automatically subtitled his words, even if they were understandable to them.

"King Asha," Torres said, as he returned the bow and the gesture. "I was wondering if you would like to take a short tour of the ship with us?"

Excitement washed over them from the alien, giving them his answer before he had even spoken in response. He turned to the two other Kuldar with him before Torres interjected carefully. "King Asha, some of the areas we will visit are only authorized for the highest-ranking members of the crew…"

Asha understood, a tiny jolt of electricity passing through their minds that felt like smugness or even a little arrogance. He spoke to his entourage, the words translating into text which both Torres and Brandt read without letting their faces show how easy it had been to manipulate the alien.

"You stay here," he told them. "Not important enough to see human ship."

"This way, please," Brandt said.

She gestured towards the door with a smile as fake as a lump of Martian rock sold in the Lunar markets. Asha donned a pair of dark goggles, which would filter out most of the higher spectrum light and protect his sensitive eyes. They weaved through the decks, all the while Torres giving facts about the ship which were so confidently delivered that Brandt couldn't be sure if he was bullshitting or not. Reaching a forward compartment where the Fold Drive emitter and shield array power source was housed, he gave Brandt the slightest of looks. She took that as the sign to begin.

"Asha, answer me something…" Torres said casually.

"Of course, Captain."

"Why are the Va'alen really here in this system?" A coldness filled the room as the alien stood tall and resolved. The question, so innocently asked, had turned the mood sour.

"I make no apologies for what my ancestors did," he said strongly

Torres noted he had avoided answering the question.

"So your people *did* start the war then?" Torres said. There was still no answer after the words were translated. "Does that also mean that the Va'alen aren't the violent… people… you made them out to be?"

A feeling resembling resolved anger filled the room. "My ancestors attacked an alien race who came to our home world and wanted war. We responded in kind."

"That doesn't answer his question, Asha," Brandt said menacingly from just behind his right shoulder. From that angle he could sense her but couldn't see her.

"We did not attack the Va'alen," he said angrily, the rapid clicking of his native words rattling so fast that they had to wait for the translation software to catch up. "The species we destroyed are *not* the Va'alen; they came afterwards and devastated our world. Forced us to flee through the gateway. Followed us and left us with only one hope that failed, and here they stayed to take the resources of this system."

"Who were the others?" Torres asked, confused.

"They were… *different.*"

"Different *how*?" Brandt asked.

"They were..." Asha hesitated. "They were like you, only not like you."

Neither of the humans sealed inside the section needed an empathic projection to know that the other felt shock at his words.

"Like *us*?" Torres asked icily.

"I cannot say for certain," Asha said carefully, worry emanating from him. "All the records of this were scrubbed from our archives by the queens who came after we were stranded here."

"So why *did* the Va'alen attack you?" the captain asked.

"This, we do not know... some believe it was retribution for our attack on the others. Some believe it was coincidence."

"What do you believe?" he asked the alien. He stepped close and looked directly into his goggled eyes.

"I believe," Asha said sadly, his emotions clear as day to them, "that the species we attacked were a subjugate of the Va'alen and came as their messengers or scouts. We travelled from our system through the gateway to here. They followed, and we have been hiding ever since."

"So the... the *portal* technology is Kuldar?" Torres challenged him.

"It was, but I do not know what it has become now. The technology was very secret, only the highest-ranking members of our race knew anything of it. We left with only one ship that used part of that technology. When that left we were stranded here with only a single ship to use. We survived with what we had, and whether you think that this is our own fault or not I beg of you not to abandon us."

Torres relented, shrinking down and dialing back the intimidation. Behind Asha, Brandt took her hand off the pistol holstered under her left arm and relaxed also.

"So," she said quietly, "you started a war and lost everything, and now you want us to side with you?"

Asha turned to face her, his facial expression revealing nothing but his feelings pinning her to the wall.

"What other choice do you have?"

Torres gave the news to the admiral in person with Brandt beside him.

He had left the *Ichi* in the hands of Sarvanto and piloted the *Tanto* himself over to the gigantic colony ship, There he could see the battered frigate being worked on by dozens of engineering crews in shuttles and performing EVAs on her outer hull. As they worked, they swarmed over her wounds like ants on a bullet-holed body. The *Tanto* had docked with permission, found an escort waiting for them and followed them directly to the bridge. The bridge easily three times as large as their own ship's. They waited outside the admiral's quarters before being admitted to the big stateroom.

"At ease," Dassiova said.

The usual uniform of a fleet admiral had been abandoned in place of the more practical flight suit the other officers also wore. Brandt noted that her former commanding officer, with his reputation of being a hard-ass and very much the soldier's soldier, wore a pistol on his right thigh.

"Sir, I thought it better we brief you in person about our conversation with the Kuldar," Torres said.

"Take a seat," he said. As he directed them, he made eye contact with Brandt and flashed a look of recognition that didn't seem friendly. "Tell me."

"In a nutshell, Admiral, the intel is partially correct," Torres said. He sat stiffly, ready to stand when the fleet commander did.

"Only partially? Lay it out for me like I'm five, son," Dassiova growled at him. He had had too long a day already to be messed around with information in small doses.

"They did start the war, only it seems by proxy; they attacked another alien race and in short order the Va'alen arrived and destroyed their home world. The gateway technology was Kuldar, but the Va'alen took it over after the survivors fled and followed them to this system. The Kuldar then sent a prototype scout ship ahead to find somewhere to go —based on the same technology as the gateway so I'm assuming that it's a static Fold Drive of sorts—only they never came back. We know why, because they crash-landed on Earth and that's wh—"

"Just the current events, Captain," Dassiova interrupted.

"Assume I've read a goddamned briefing docket before I came all the way out here."

"Sorry, sir," Torres said quickly. "So it looks like there is or at least *was* another alien race who the Kuldar described as looking a little like us. That the tech we all use to defeat the physics of spacetime all originated in the same place at one point."

"So we're in the middle of someone else's war and we have inadvertently picked sides?" the admiral asked testily.

"Seems so, sir."

"Well, shit," he answered. "And now our options are to limp home, having half-destroyed a few trillion credits of prototype fleet ships with a few hundred alien refugees, or what? Dive right into their war?"

"Sir," Brandt said as she leaned forward, "it's not for us to tell the admiral what to do b—"

"You're absolutely, unequivocally, goddamned *right* it's not," Dassiova said. The tone of his voice was so low and controlled that it would have been far less intimidating for him to draw his weapon and pointed it at her head.

She continued tentatively. "But I imagine that would be a decision for our command back on Earth to make. All I'm saying is that the tech advances and the resources on offer in this system are worth a little risk to keep exploring."

"Your opinion," Dassiova said with mock deference, "is duly noted, Commander. Did it occur to you to that I also have a functioning brain and I, being the fleet admiral, might even be privy to information that you two renegades aren't? You know the sensor readings from the drones have been transmitted back to Earth and the eggheads back there are having a fit just thinking about the raw materials?"

Torres and Brandt exchanged a brief look as Dassiova went on.

"The way Earth sees it," he said, "it doesn't make a damned bit of difference who pissed on whose yard first; this system either is or isn't worth the risk of exploring for resources. They believe that it is. The real question remains, *can we win?*" He banged a fist down onto the desktop as he spoke and startled them both by the suddenness and loudness of the gesture.

"Well, sir…" Torres began.

"Rhetorical question, Torres, pipe down and you may yet learn something," Dassiova told him. "If these Kuldar are good for their word that they can give us advanced tech which we will be sharing with all of the territories back home. There will be a combined fleet in this sector in as little as six months. That's how long it would take to retrofit just about every big ship we have, and all of those ships better be sporting the most insanely powerful alien ray guns available if we have a hope in hell of defeating the bastards who attacked us. We will *not* seek a diplomatic resolution with the Va'alen, but the fact remains that while that gateway device is still operational they can bring infinite reinforcements through, as far as we know."

He paused for a moment, lending gravity to his next words.

"We need to destroy that device, bring back the Kuldar refugees and then return with a bigger fleet to mop up what's left of them, which, from what our probes are telling us, is a hell of a lot more than we've already faced."

Brandt and Torres sat back in stunned silence. "So, what do you need from us, sir?"

CHAPTER 18

Proxima Centauri B Orbit

"How many more?" the Master Petty Officer yelled through his suit's speakers at the seamen at the foot of the dropship ramp.

In helpful answer, which he realized would guarantee him an ass-chewing later, the seaman shrugged unhelpfully back up the ramp as the line of nervous aliens trudged past him.

Even though they had been briefed, the troops from the *Venture* were totally taken aback by the sudden influx of unexpected emotions they felt when in proximity to the Kuldar. Nervous tension cramped their muscles, elevated their heart rates and made managing the evacuation an almost impossible task. Their unit commanders sat inside the command centers onboard the dropships that had settled in three different locations on the habitable ring of the dull, red-bathed planet. They watched as the bio-sign readouts of their troops spiked and dipped at such an alarming rate that twice the operation had almost been cancelled and the vessels returned to their mothership. They had followed orders and stayed the course.

They were refugees; scared and nervous about the arrival of the new aliens who had fought with the enemy of their people. Refugees who now faced uncertainty at the mercy of these same aliens whom their leaders had placed total trust in for the very survival of their entire race.

Little wonder why the armed soldiers, placed to line their route, appeared only as metal humanoids with reflective plates where their faces should be. As they passed the soldiers, the population of thin-limbed, large-headed aliens looked at them with fear and wonder in their big eyes. They carried weapons and gave off no emotions, so they sparked fear in the young and the old of the Kuldar, despite the assurances from their queen that they were to trust in her and go with the metal people.

Most of them had never set foot inside a spacecraft, had never even seen one. Their people possessed only the single ship, which had been left behind by their ancestors. Only the queen and her inner circle had ever taken that ship off-world, and even that had run the risk of bringing the Va'alen down on them. It was the arrival of these aliens that had done that; had brought a swarm of Va'alen to the skies above the ring of life on their planet. Two of the demons had landed on their world and fought with the newcomers. Rumor had spread that those two Va'alen had destroyed a legion of the metal people before they blew themselves up to demonstrate their power. These rumors, wildly exaggerated with each excited retelling, had served only to increase the spreading fear and panic among the Kuldar.

"We're at capacity," shouted the master petty officer. He waved at the advancing line of Kuldar to stop where they were. The aliens were holding all the belongings they could carry, and shuffled to a halt. A few moments of panic ensued when family groups were separated either side of the cut-off line. Some ran back from the dropship to reunite with family members. The senior NCO lost his temper and took off while the ship was still under capacity. He was impatient and couldn't cajole them to fill every seat. He gave up, and as one ship rose high into the sky, another swooped in to settle down and drop its own cargo ramp. Another armor-suited alien waved the Kuldar forward to climb the sloping metal and take seats in the strange craft taking them to unknown and frightening new places.

"It is alright," a soothing Kuldar voice said over their frightened mutterings. "We will all be together on their ships, and we will be together on a new world where the Va'alen cannot find us."

They shuffled forward, reassured by the words of one of their senior leaders placed among the people to keep them calm.

The *Ichi* was already at capacity. Their only vacant cargo hold had been filled with close to a hundred Kuldar—the queen, her husband and family at the heart of the small community there. The basic needs of the aliens—food, water and waste recycling—had hastily been met with the retrofitting, but the Kuldar on the *Ichi* had been specially selected for their engineering knowledge and ability. They didn't have much in the way of possessions, but what they did have seemed paltry in comparison to the almost obsessive human attachment to possessions.

These few, the engineering vanguard, were hard at work alongside the scientists and engineers of the human crew. They were all tasked with developing the integration of technology between the two alien races and working on the biggest problem: how to make the two systems interface.

The primary objective, according to orders from Earth, was the development and implementation of an advanced weapons system.

⁓

Torres was pissed.

He had jumped to command, undoubtedly too early in his career, only to find himself the captain of a ship mere minutes later. Such a jump was unheard of. It was circumstance and a healthy dose of luck—good or bad depending on how anyone looked at it—that led to the set of occurrences that put him in command. He hadn't had that command stripped from him, not yet, even when the four ships and their respective captains, who all had far greater experience than he did, arrived from their home system.

Dassiova, a man with a fearsome reputation, had left him in command of the *Ichi*. In private, the admiral had told him how he had done a good job and achieved the mission, even if he had a number of 'developmental issues' to address with him when they were safely back in home waters.

After that, he had heard nothing. He had been, to use the seaman's vernacular, totally and utterly 'mushroomed.' He'd been kept in the dark and fed bullshit.

No further orders came, no communication to or from Earth was put through, and everything he needed to know was filtered down from the admiral. Torres wasn't a renegade at heart and was certainly no maverick soldier hell-bent on doing things his own way, but he was finding himself increasingly pissed at being left out of the loop.

I may be young, he thought to himself as he paced his quarters, *maybe even too young to have a command like this, but hasn't my record shown me to be competent? Haven't I achieved my own success with nothing to do with family connections or privilege? So why am I not being involved in the big picture?*

He decided to seek his own answers to that and left the bridge. He was accompanied by a man Torres had fetched personally. Together they walked to the cargo bay where the guarding soldiers of his crew admitted him access. There he greeted the Kuldar by returning the gestures of their bowed heads and their fingertips touching their foreheads before they spoke. The man Torres had brought with him moved behind him reluctantly, either because of the early hour or a fear of the alien race. Torres heavily suspected it was the lack of sleep that caused the lagging in his steps; he had known the man to be awful at getting his ass out of bed even seven years earlier.

"Are my people from the other ship here?" he asked the Kuldar.

"No," the Kuldar greeting him said excitedly. "You are the only one of your people here."

"Good," Torres said. "Is Asha here?"

He was led to the alien who had made first contact with his crew and found him working over holographic plans projected in orange light, which were swiped away when he approached.

"Asha," Torres said, "I have brought one of the best minds of my people to work with yours. Asha, this is Doctor Paterson."

Paterson stepped forward, awkwardly bowing stiffly, and then touching his thumb and forefinger to his forehead in greeting.

"How can I help you, Healer Paterson?" Asha asked, the translation device misinterpreting his words.

"Not that kind of doctor," Paterson said. "I'm a scientist."

Asha checked the translation. "How can I help you, Scientist Paterson?"

"The captain and I had a little idea," Paterson said, "and it's one that needs whatever tech you're running on your ship."

Asha's face registered confusion; some of Paterson's words hadn't translated properly.

"Try not to use any abbreviations or metaphors when talking to them," Torres said quietly. "It confuses the software; it's only programmed about forty-five percent of language so far."

Paterson nodded in small apology.

"We need the device you use on your ship to mask your readings," he explained. "I think I know a way to improve it."

"Improve it?" Asha asked. "How?"

"We detected you by your energy signature," Torres explained, "because it's almost the same as ours. We use the same kind of energy source as you do. Paterson here thinks he can modulate the energy output to the same frequency as your disruption device."

"The shroud?" Asha asked. Their best approximation would have called it a cloak, but translating as 'shroud' made sense. Nobody liked the words 'cloaking device;' it felt a little too fictional, despite their sudden appearance in a place that felt almost entirely fictional.

"Yes," Torres said. "Can you give us access to it?"

Asha bowed his head slightly as if in thought. They both felt a wave of apprehension, perhaps even a slight amount of fear, as he spoke the next words.

"This I cannot do without permission from my queen, and she will want to know what you need this for."

"Well…" Torres said. He seemed apprehensive, as if he was about to admit to breaking his grandmother's favorite vase. "That's where it might get a little… *sticky.*"

⁓

"You want to do *what?*" Admiral Dassiova yelled as he stood from his chair and slammed both hands on his desk. "Are you out of your mind, *Captain?*"

"No, sir," Torres said. He stood still and to attention; the tried and tested method of surviving an ass-chewing from a senior officer. "If the admiral would just hear me out—"

"Hear the rest of your suicide mission that involves the intentional destruction of a billion-credits' worth of warship under my command? Have you even considered what the captain of the proposed ship is going to do to you?"

"Yes, sir, I have. At length. The way I see it is this," he said, speaking quickly before the admiral chewed him out again, "the fleet is under-gunned and too damaged to risk a head-on fight with the Va'alen. If we just left the system for six months or a year, then we would lose the foothold and be facing unknown enemy numbers when we returned. We know we can't take them on hand-to-hand without heavy losses unless we use battle mechs; even those will need some serious upgrades to get the job done. You said it yourself, Admiral, that gateway represents infinite enemy reinforcements and we need to take it out. I believe that the risk versus reward stakes are high enough to sacrifice a wounded frigate."

Dassiova sat heavily and stared at the young man. Torres had risen from a smooth-faced boy in one of his peacekeeper units to a UNID-attached commander who somehow managed to end up in command of one of the most important missions in Earth history. The admiral held his breath, honestly not knowing whether the kid was insane, arrogant, or brilliant, and let it out in an exhausted sigh. He leaned back and rubbed his face, trying to remember the last time he'd grabbed more than an hour's sleep.

"Let's just agree that I'm willing to humor this little fantasy of yours, Torres," he said more quietly. "Tell me the plan."

"Sir!" Captain Halstead protested, her eyes glistening with tears of rage at her frustration. She wanted to let rip on the very junior captain; killing him with her bare hands in front of the fleet admiral would certainly be outside the doctrine of military discipline. Her Australian accent grew more pronounced when she was angry, and right then she was very angry. "You want to give *him* my ship, just so he can intentionally destroy it?"

"Hold your horses," Dassiova said. "Look at the bigger picture here. I know the *Norton* is your baby and you *know* that I know you've captained her exceptionally, but we need to face facts; she's too damaged to make the series of jumps required to make it home unless she's dependent on the *Venture* as she is now. What Captain Torres is proposing is a way to achieve the mission, make our next mission viable, and get us all home safe and sound, where—" the admiral held up a hand to stop the interruption that was about to explode from her mouth, "— where I will ensure that you and your crew are given the next warship fresh out of the shipyard. Hell, you can even rename her the *Norton's Revenge* if you like."

Nicola Halstead shut her mouth, then opened it again to push her luck.

"In that case, I want to command the mission."

Dassiova readied, aimed, and fired his trademark glare. She didn't falter one bit under his oppressive stare, which perturbed him a little.

"You are aware that this is this the UNPF? That I'm still the fleet admiral and that you are still a frigate captain?" he asked her dangerously.

"Yes, sir, I am. I also formally request that my crew fulfill the *Norton's* final mission."

"If I say 'granted,'" Dassiova asked stiffly, "will you stop eye-balling me like that?"

"Yes, sir."

"You can command the mission, but Captain Torres will be your second-in-command and your crew will be a skeleton crew sufficient only to pilot the *Norton* into position before you make your escape back here and we can all go home for medals."

"And you can guarantee that I'll be back with the next fleet with a new ship?" she asked, pressing her advantage.

"I cannot guarantee anything, Captain," Dassiova said testily. "But you have my word that I will do everything in my power to make good on what I offered. This is the UN; we're not pirates who can just make our ransom demands. I have to sell it to the powers-that-be based on the heroism and selfless sacrifice of you and your crew."

Silence hung in the room as Halstead turned to fire a full broadside of stink-eye at Torres.

"You better tell me your plan then, *Commander.*"

CHAPTER 19

Deep Orbit of Alpha Centauri

Eight Days Later

They had made a four-minute jump to get from the dull red dwarf at the fringes of the system to the brighter of the twin suns. From that deep space infiltration point they travelled half a million kilometers until Torres called an all-stop.

"Power everything down," he said softly. "Activate the shroud."

The *Ichi* went into emergency power mode. Paterson had suggested this when he had retrofitted the device copied from the Kuldar's small ship and aligned it to their main power source and shield generator. All pieces now hummed the same tune.

"Tactical: give me passive long-range sensor sweeps at minimum intervals."

The officer at the tactical station aye-aye'd him and tapped at the screen. The passive sensors were reactive only, but to use their active sensor pulses would be to ring the dinner gong for any Va'alen in the sector. Beside him, radiating anger that didn't require the projective telepathic power of the Kuldar to detect, sat Captain Halstead.

"How long do we wait?" she asked, criticism heavy in her words.

Torres doubted that she would ever forgive him for his plan to intentionally destroy her ship.

"Tactical?" he said without actually answering her. It was *his* bridge after all. "Time to the gateway device and the Va'alen hub at non-FTL from here?"

"Stand by."

"A little over three hours, sir."

"We wait three and a half hours," Torres announced.

"Then we can move." Halstead took a long breath in through her nose and let it out. Such a sigh spoke more about her feelings for Torres than mere words could have achieved.

After two hours sitting in the dull silence at battle stations, Torres ordered the teams on the gun positions to rotate. Halstead shot him a questioning look.

"Fresh eyes," he responded. "Need to stay sharp. And two hours looking down the HUD sights on alert saps a person's strength."

Halstead huffed slightly, unclear as to whether she was dismissing his orders as frivolous or unnecessary, or whether she begrudgingly accepted the logic in them.

"You served much time as a ground-pounder?" Torres asked her quietly, trying to make conversation.

Halstead turned to answer but hesitated. "You tell me. You've read my file, right? You UNID types like to know all the details about your allies."

"Who said I was UNID?" he asked. She merely raised an eyebrow to dismiss his question as a stupid one.

"I've not had that pleasure," he said in a tone that he intended to be smooth but came across as a little aloof. "I've not had reason to."

He could have accessed her confidential personnel report at any time given his UNID clearance levels. If he really wanted to, he could get to the really juicy bits that are redacted from almost every other security access level, like the transcripts from mandatory psych reports and access to personal comm device records.

"I…" She hesitated again, then continued brusquely as if the information she was about to give was of no consequence. "I went to sea as a lieutenant. Comm and helm specialisms. Never went back to the units."

"So, you've been doing Red Runs and lunar patrols all this time?"

"No," she said, not bothering to hide her annoyance at his words. "I've been doing deep-system reconnaissance missions, running security for science vessels as well."

"Nice," Torres said. "So when did you get the *Norton*?"

"Listen, asshole," she hissed at him. Her temper finally broke when his casual small talk mentioned the ship she was about to lose.

"Contact detected!" the tactical officer reported.

Both captains looked to the displays beside their chairs. The officer called out the bearing and put it on screen. Nothing showed, only the faintest ripples as the cloaked ships distorted the light of a few distant stars.

"Just one contact," Torres said, "but we can assume that's a small pack of four Va'alen ships. People, it's safe to say that they can detect the presence of a ship jumping in but don't have FTL capability in their small ships. Keep an eye on them, Tac. I want to know if they get our scent and head this way."

"And if they do?" Halstead asked Torres.

"What would you suggest?" She snorted, knowing that he was intentionally blowing

smoke up her ass when he could've just given the answer.

"Then we jump towards the objective, ping as many active sensor sweeps as we can before they launch fighters at us, and jump back out."

"Good plan." Torres smiled at her, infuriating her even further. He knew he should lay off, should stop goading the fierce Australian woman.

He had resisted the urge to pull her file, even when he found himself with a small window of time within the previous week that had been a manic rush of constant, round-the-clock work. They had fitted the shroud to the *Ichi* with surprisingly few problems. That in itself sparked fear—if something was too easy, then it was probably wrong. The team took it all apart and refitted everything on his orders to be absolutely certain. When they tested it, they found only a ten percent drop in auxiliary power and had hailed the *Venture* to see if they had her on any sensors. They tested everything for a day and a half; how fast they could travel before they were visible, what sensors they could use without showing an energy reading in a ship actively looking for them. They fired weapons to see how visible that made them, and eventually they came up with a protocol to be followed when shrouded.

Dassiova, despite his nature and his position, was impressed. Both with the technology and with how fast the engineers in his fleet had built and retrofitted it to the recon ship.

He ordered the team responsible for it, under the leadership of a scientist who had also served under him long ago, to ship immediately to the *Venture* where they could join the other teams working constantly to fix up the *Norton* and fit her with the same kind of device.

He had ordered every supply, almost every round of heavy ship ammunition and all but two of her remaining guns to be offloaded. The crew had been pressed into temporary service elsewhere with the majority going to the *Hammer* to best utilize their expertise with frigates.

Halstead had made a promise to her crew. They had conducted a ceremony in which they honored the dead, burying those at sea for whom they had bodies and remembering those whose lives had ended horribly when the decks lost containment and they were sucked into the vacuum of space. She had promised them a new ship, to be reunited with the rest of the surviving crewmembers, and she had promised them that *she* would be back with them, by whatever means necessary. They had cheered her, humbling the other captains with a crew's dedication to their leader. She had stepped down from the podium with only the most fleeting of dirty looks being fired at Torres.

"Sir, it looks like they're... *de-cloaking*...?" the tactical officer said uncertainly.

"On screen," Torres ordered, standing to take a pace toward the large display. There he saw four of the Va'alen ships split apart and fly in different directions in pairs.

"Why do they shroud as one?" Halstead asked as she stepped up beside him.

"I do not know," Torres mused slowly. "Perhaps they have to combine their fields or something? Perhaps it's tactical?"

"Whatever," Halstead answered. "There's your answer; they can't find any breadcrumbs to follow. Helm? Set a course fo—" She stopped, turning to look at Torres with a mixture of apology and shock as she had fallen into the command she had held naturally for so long.

"I apologize, Captain," she said quietly but humbly.

"No apology necessary," Torres muttered back to her. He had only been a captain for a few weeks but already the ship and her crew felt like his children. He could not imagine how bad it would feel when they got back, and he found himself demoted in place of a more experienced leader.

"Set a course for the gateway, one-half speed," he ordered, erring on the side of caution. He knew they could travel at close to three-quarters speed without detection.

"Course laid in, sir," the helmsman responded. "ETA seven hours and forty minutes."

"Good work," Torres said aloud to the bridge. "Tac, you keep a close eye on those bugs and call me if any of them head after us. Mister Sarvanto, you have the bridge. Remind Commander Brandt to rotate the gunners every two hours."

He turned to Halstead, gesturing for her to lead on toward the captain's cabin. She nodded her thanks and stepped confidently through the doors. Torres followed, pouring coffee into two mugs from the permanently lukewarm pot that he never quite figured out how to turn up.

"You stayed a ground-pounder, didn't you?" she asked him as she sipped her drink and winced at the temperature.

Torres sipped his own and pulled a similar face, holding out a hand for her cup to throw them both into the small sink and start a fresh pot.

"Yeah, I actually served under Dassiova on the lunar surface about eight years ago when that big terror attack happened," he said. "I was a fresh ensign then, and man was I scared..."

His honesty intrigued her, and she leaned back to regard him with something resembling fresh eyes.

"And after that?" she asked.

"After that I got shipped back to Earth, got a medal for shooting a terrorist when I wasn't even sure I had my eyes open when I pulled the trigger. Got a bump to LT through OTA Colima." He paused, decanting the instant coffee into two cups and sitting back down opposite her. "After that I trained and studied harder than ever and made CP. Hit lieutenant commander after another three years, not that the rank mattered in CP as I was still working for a Chief PO but at least the pay increased some. I did a few Red Runs and qualified for command at sea, went back home and got my own CP command and then… I got posted elsewhere."

"You got drafted by UNID," Halstead said, accepting the fresh cup and levelling the statement as an accusation.

"As a UN military advisor."

"As a spook," she shot back.

Torres chewed the inside of his cheek as he ran through his available options of responses. He chose to move on and ignore the comment.

"And now I'm here," he said. "I made commander on a technicality so as to be in mission command prior to the test flights for the *Ichi* and when it all hit the fan on the moon I was the ranking officer onboard."

"But you weren't, though, were you? Brandt is the senior commander, isn't she?" Again, her question was an arrow-straight statement of fact.

"Yes, but she never qualified for ship command, because she chose CP instead."

"Yeah, to avoid doing waste runs in charge of a tub taking dried pasta to Mars with two lame troops under her command…"

Seeing Torres's expression in response to her mockery made her think that she'd made a mistake by insulting the woman who everyone knew was a fast-tracked officer candidate. Like other tracks, Brandt had attracted scorn everywhere she went. Nobody thought she'd stick around long enough to care about those under her command before she got shipped to the next job. It was well known that when tracks hit rank they were usually pushed off into political roles ready to leave the service and take up office somewhere, but those who weren't that connected usually faced the worst commands in the solar system.

"I..." Halstead began before trailing off.

"Leslie Brandt is an outstanding soldier who is totally committed to the corps and her mission. She's an asset to my crew, and she's my friend. You know we served together on the moon when the terrorists attacked us? You know she took a few bullets for that and earned her way into OTA with me? There are tracks and there are *tracks*. She's a fine commander and you'd do much worse than to have someone like her in charge of your ground-pounders."

"I'm sorry, Kyle," she said, surprising him that she even knew his first name. "I didn't mean to cause offence. I didn't know you were close."

Another accusation tinged her words and Torres's eyes narrowed slightly.

"It's not that, either," he told her.

She was saved having to respond when the buzzer sounded from his door.

"Yeah," he yelled informally into the intercom that automatically came to life when the door was buzzed. He continued to surprise the older captain with how easy he took to ship command. In walked a beautiful young woman with soft brown skin so smooth it didn't seem natural. She was dressed in armor minus the helmet and bore the insignia of the CP teams with *Viper* stenciled on her right breast.

She even looks like a Viper, Halstead thought.

The woman walked in speaking but stopped and stared at Halstead like she was a target as she sat comfortably opposite the captain.

"My apologies, Captain," she said in an African accent much softened by living in a different territory; probably Britain if Halstead's ears were to be trusted. "I did not know you had company. I will leave."

"No, Eze, it's fine. Lieutenant Amare Eze, Captain Nicola Halstead."

Halstead stood, offering her hand to the suited but still petite soldier who was a head shorter than her. Eze seemed to hesitate for a fraction of a second, then shook the hand and smiled her greetings. Her eyes didn't mirror the smile, which Halstead always looked for. The grip of the powered armor was only slightly uncomfortable to her, but she let it slide.

"I will speak to you later, Captain," she said, giving them both a nod and dismissing herself by walking out of the room. As the door hissed shut behind her, Halstead turned to raise another eyebrow at Torres.

Torres didn't meet her gaze and seemed to shift awkwardly in his seat as he cleared his throat.

"Personal visit, was it?" she needled him gently.

"What?"

"Your lieutenant? She didn't have anything to report?" A smile crept across her lips; she couldn't contain what the most basic of female intuition had detected.

"I'm sure it wasn't an important matter," Torres said in a tone that was as dismissive as it was unconvincing. "Now if you'll excuse me, I need a few hours' sleep before I take the next rotation."

Halstead finished her coffee, placing the cup down carefully as she swallowed the last gulp.

"I'll do the same," she said as she stood and smoothed down her flight suit. "See you back on the bridge in six hours."

CHAPTER 20

Orbit of Earth-Like Planet

"Can we risk sending out the new sensor probe?" Halstead asked Torres.

Torres thought the question was worth exploring and asked his tactical officer.

"Not sure, sir," she replied. "The velocity of the launch is close to the speed of the warheads and they were detected by the *Venture* when we tested the shroud."

"Can we override the launch burn and use maneuvering thrusters only?"

"Not without taking the probe apart, sir…"

"What about a soft launch?" Brandt asked. She had joined the bridge, still in her replacement armor courtesy of the big colony ship. She had to remain ready to do her job in an instant.

"Could work…" Torres mused. "Tactical, open the probe launch doors and prepare to release the clamps. Helm, line us up with the planet and stand by for all ahead stop."

Both stations reported ready. Torres gave the command and watched the display beside him as the two stations worked in tandem. The free probe was a version of their warheads that ran on charged battery power instead of carrying a singularity.

That singularity was usually both weapon and power source. This one, however, carried a full sensor array in place of the targeting and detonation equipment and slid from the tube to slip ahead of their suddenly stationary ship.

"Probe launched," the tactical officer reported. "Engaging thrusters now."

"Excellent," Torres said. "How long does it need to soak?" The sooner the small projectile would take to orbit the planet and transmit the sensor data to them the better.

"A little over an hour and twenty, sir."

Their fleet had previously sent out long-range probes, the unimaginably expensive single-use ones with miniature Fold Drives and subspace comm arrays. What they had not detected before they had been picked up and destroyed was the planet on the far side of the bigger of the twin suns in the system. They suspected there was a planet there, because the Kuldar intelligence suggested that the Va'alen were mining for resources, but they hadn't been able to get a close enough look.

They looked at it at maximum magnification. The collective gasp that ran through the bridge had them all staring at the display. It was Earth—not *their* Earth but a planet so similar that without looking closely at the shapes of the continental plates, none of them could say that they weren't looking at their own planet.

Torres had brought up one of the science team to the bridge, a cosmologist who was onboard to map the system as accurately as possible from the sensor data they received. His opinion made for a simple explanation.

"There's nothing overly unique about our planet," he said. "Just the formation of land masses which have changed entirely over a relatively short period of time—short in galactic terms anyway. You're aware of the concept of the goldilocks band?"

Torres was. It was space colonization 101 for anyone actually going out there. Being the right distance from the sun to allow for liquid water to exist was the basis of planetary life. His expression told the scientist to try not to patronize him.

"Well, this planet appears about the same size and mass as our own but is a little further away from the sun."

"But that sun is bigger than ours," Torres pointed out.

"Precisely, which evens out to provide the same kind of conditions. I'd wager it's almost a replica of Earth, so long as no stinky humans have poisoned it."

"Facts, not opinions," Torres reminded him.

"Sorry," he said. "When your probe sends back the data, I think we'll be looking at a viable planet to populate."

He left out his thought about the option of stripping it bare and burning all of the natural resources to set the timer on that viability expiring. Torres thanked him and politely dismissed him from the bridge as they sat and waited for the probe to return. It was technically outside of their mission parameters, but having expended the energy and resources to infiltrate so far into enemy-held territory, Torres would have felt remiss not to investigate, just so long as it didn't compromise their primary objective.

"Tactical, can we see the Va'alen hub from here?" he asked.

"No, sir, it's on the other side of Alpha Centauri from us."

Torres chewed the inside of his lip. He mulled over his options and found no way to safely cut the corners. They would just have to deal with a delay of an hour before resuming the mission.

"Stay on the sensors," he told his crew. "I don't want any surprises while we're camped out here."

~

"Any sign of them yet?" Admiral Dassiova asked his bridge crew. They were using active sensors, given that the enemy already knew they were there, and as a precaution were all lined up pointing out of the system ready to jump if any overwhelming force threatened them. The *Ichi* was now light years away on reconnaissance, a job she had been built for, although now enhanced tenfold with the retrofitted addition of the alien shroud device. Dassiova much preferred shroud device to a cloaking field, as someone had wanted to name it, and decided to stick with the translation of the alien word for the hardware.

"Nothing yet, sir," one of his crew called out in response. "Do you want to hail them?"

Dassiova turned to stare at the young man who had spoken.

"You ever play hide and seek as a kid?" he asked casually.

"Err, I guess..." the young man answered.

"You ever shout out to your other buddies hiding when the kid looking for you was around?"

"Understood, sir, sorry."

"Dumbass," the admiral muttered not quite under his breath. He was contemplating kicking the kid off his bridge for medal-winning stupidity, but settled on that being a too harsh. He had made his point.

An excited shout made the admiral jump in his chair.

"Fold Drive signal detected!" They waited in impatient anticipation of the next words. "It's the *Ichi*. She's hailing you directly, Admiral."

"On screen," he growled.

Torres's face blinked into life on the main display with Halstead's just beside it.

"Captains," Dassiova said in gruff greeting.

"Admiral," Torres said intensely. "We've accomplished the mission and then some, but we now have a ticking clock."

CHAPTER 21

Deep Space Near Proxima Centauri

"So, you're telling me there's a viable Earth-like planet on the far side of this system?" the admiral asked the two tired-looking captains seated opposite him in his main briefing room.

"Yes, sir," Halstead answered, pushing a datapad across the wide table towards him. "Atmospheric readings from the probe show it to have the same gas components as our own, only a little richer and with almost none of the pollution we have in ours."

Dassiova grunted as he read the report. He didn't actually know the percentage composition of Earth's atmosphere off the top of his head but decided not to announce his ignorance.

"And what about the primary mission objective?"

"Achieved, sir," Torres said. "But I need to report in reverse order. We have a threat incoming, and it isn't one that we can withstand."

"Don't just sit there looking pretty, Torres. Spit it out!"

~

After the probe had done a seemingly lazy lap of the planet from high in the atmosphere, the officer controlling it from the tactical station engaged the engine and maneuvering thrusters just the right amount to break it out of atmosphere and send it back towards them.

Deciding it was best not to risk discovery by retrieving the entire probe, and also because he was anxious to get on with the mission, the tactical officer ordered the data be downloaded remotely and then had the probe set on a course to burn up in the larger of the two suns.

"Set a course for the gateway device," he ordered the helm. "Half speed."

"Aye, aye, sir, our time to contact is…" he dragged out the word as it was calculating, "one hour fifteen."

"Understood," Torres acknowledged before hitting the ship-wide transmission channel. "All hands, this is the Captain. Remain at battle stations; we are approaching the objective in one hour. Torres out."

Tense silence filled the bridge, as it likely did on the other decks in nervous anticipation of their mission to sneak into the enemy's back yard.

An hour seemed to take far longer than under almost any other circumstance. That was how it felt to the captain, sitting in his chair the entire time and trying not to show how nervous he truly was. He especially didn't want to seem anxious in front of the more experienced Captain Halstead. He could have watched a couple of old reruns of his favorite shows in that time. He could have read a book or even grabbed himself a precious bit of rack time, but none of those things was even a remote possibility under the conditions. The seconds ticked down agonizingly until an unexpected curse came from beside him.

"Well, smack my ass," Halstead blurted out. She suddenly remembered herself and fought the flush of color rising in her cheeks. "That planet—it's just like home."

She had been reviewing the sensor data from the probe, something Torres had all but forgotten about, and pointed at his console so that he could review it himself.

"Well I'll be damned," he muttered. "Well *this* certainly changes things. There's no way Earth will give up on this system now."

"There's more," Halstead told him. She continued to look down at the screen beside her. "It's got animal life—I mean there are life-sign readings all over the planet, but there's no evidence of structures or anything to say that higher-evolved lifeforms are there."

"So... like Earth but *younger?*" Torres asked. "In evolutionary terms, I mean."

"Could be."

"I wonder if—" Torres started to say before a shout cut him off.

"Contact! Dead ahead!" shouted the tactical officer.

"Calm yourself," Torres said in a low voice. He forced himself not to sound as frightened and excited as the young officer was. "Report."

"I'm reading two—no, *three* readings. The same kind of energy reading as the Va'alen ships."

"Distance?" Torres asked.

"Twelve thousand kilometers and closing, sir. I don't know how they got so close without us detecting them."

"They came around the sun," Rogers said from the helm. "They were masked by the solar radiation."

"What's their trajectory?" Torres asked, shifting in his seat and trying not to sound worried.

"Err...uh..." the tactical officer said. "Err..."

"Take your time," he told him. "Get it right."

"It looks like an intercept course, sir," he said. "But they're going to overshoot us at our current speed."

"I am of the opinion that their course could be a coincidence," Torres said, glancing at Halstead to see if she agreed with his gut feeling. She gave the slightest nod in support. He was careful not to show his bridge crew that he was looking to someone else for answers.

"All ahead stop. Monitor them to see if they change course. Signal the guns to be ready but *not* to fire without my express order. Get a confirmation on that. And lay in jump coordinates out of here just to be safe."

"Aye, aye, sir," chorused the officers manning the tactical, helm and comm stations.

Ten agonizing seconds passed until the report came back to him.

"No change to speed or direction, Captain," he said with obvious relief.

"Extend their trajectory and check it against our point of entry after jump," Torres ordered.

"Yep, that's where they're heading," the tactical officer responded. He suddenly remembered himself, sat more upright and added a hasty, "Sir," on the end.

"Resume course," the captain ordered. "Guns to stand down; get those safety catches back on. Let the Va'alen go poking around in empty space; that should keep them busy."

The next ten minutes to target went by more quickly, as though the win of remaining undetected had lifted the veil of nervousness stifling the air on the bridge.

"Gateway device in visual range, Captain."

"Let's see it," he said. All eyes turned to the large display. The gateway came into view, only half of it visible as the angle of it caught the sun side-on and highlighted the nearest, massive curve of the ring floating in space.

"Reminds me of a game I played once…" the young tactical officer murmured.

"Passive scans?" Torres prompted, refocusing on the kid he was about to have replaced if he didn't get his act together.

"Yes, sir," the young man snapped, almost jumping in his chair as his concentration was forced back to his job. "No cloaked readings around the device… some readings farther ahead but… no, can't detect anything on passive for certain. We're in the clear."

"Take us in, one quarter speed," Torres ordered. He leaned forward in his chair. "I want to see how close we can get without triggering any defense protocols. Keep an eye on that console, Ensign. I do *not* want any power surges spooling up without knowing about it; that thing might have weapons or some kind of point defense guns. In fact, Mister Sarvanto, would you mind relieving the young ensign? I'm sure he needs a bottle or a nap."

"Aye, sir," Sarvanto replied, the tone of his voice making it clear that he didn't care for Torres mocking one of the crew in front of everyone.

Torres heard it after he had said it. He softened the blow with his next words.

"Ensign, stay with Mister Sarvanto and watch what he does."

The kid smiled and nodded, returning to his station as an observer.

"Is it shielded?" Halstead asked as she too leaned forward to see the unusual and massive device.

"Not as far as I can see, ma'am," Sarvanto reported.

"Keep jump coordinates locked-in," Torres said. "I don't want any surprises."

His order was acknowledged by the helm. They crept closer at what, in the void of space, was a slow speed but on the surface of a planet would tear trees out of the ground with the force of their passing.

"One thousand kilometers," the helmsman called out.

"Still no sign of shields or energy surges," Sarvanto echoed.

"Keep her steady," Torres said, not knowing what he meant but pleased to be sounding *captainy* and reassuring.

"Five hundred kilometers."

"Still all clear," Sarvanto said.

"Hold us at fifty kilometers," Torres ordered.

"All stop, fifty kilometers from target," the helmsman said in a low, controlled voice as though speaking loudly could get them caught.

"Passive sensors?" Torres asked.

"It appears to be dormant," Sarvanto answered. "No enemy readings."

Torres glanced at Halstead.

"Worth risking an active sensor ping?" she asked. Torres shook his head.

"I don't want them knowing that this is our target and covering it with guns before we're back," he said a low voice. Halstead nodded, adding the ground-pounder's SpecOps playbook to her own for future use.

"Okay, set us a course back to empty space where we can jump," he ordered. "Keep us slow until we've put five thousand kilometers between us and the gateway, then go to two-thirds speed."

"Aye, aye," came the soft response from the helm. The shrouded *Ichi* turned slowly about and drifted away. They travelled unmolested away from the device, choosing not to head past it to approach the Va'alen hub—that could wait until there were far more ships on their side and within firing range. Instead, they chose a different spot of empty void to jump from, seeing as there were at least a dozen enemy ships scouring that sector last they saw. At what Torres believed was a safe distance, and far enough away from the gateway device, he ordered the jump back to the fleet in two short hops.

"Take us halfway," he told the helmsman. "Then recalculate and jump closer to the fleet."

He didn't risk sending a subspace comm to the admiral— their intel confirmed that the Va'alen could detect the energy signal of a jump, which meant they may be capable of detecting their long-range comms.

"Jump ready, sir."

"Hit it."

"Contact!" Sarvanto said loudly. He immediately added in a voice laced with more than a touch of hysteria, "Correction, *contacts*. Lots of them."

"Where?" Torres barked.

"Eight thousand kilometers to our rear... there are... there are too many to count. I'm reading them as one massive contact with others that keep breaking off from the fringes constantly."

"Speed and heading?"

"Fast, can't say for certain but I estimate that they are travelling at close to our flank speed."

"*Heading?*" Torres prompted again, allowing his fear to rule his mouth.

"Working on it," Sarvanto said as his fingertips danced across the terminal's glass surface. "Heading is… heading leads directly back towards the fleet, Captain."

"Plot a jump," Torres said. "RFN."

"Jump ready," the helmsman reported.

"Do it *now*."

―

"Unknown numbers heading our way then?" Dassiova asked, a hint of tiredness in his words.

"Yes, sir," Torres said as he swallowed down the lump in his throat. "We estimate that we have maybe sixteen hours to jump away before they're in this sector. Our best guess is they sent a sizeable force after we destroyed their forces in this sector."

Dassiova leaned forward to rest his elbows on the desk and rubbed his temples. "Are we ready to launch the *Norton*?"

"In three hours," Captain Halstead answered.

"And how long to complete that mission and get back here?" the admiral asked. He could already guess he wouldn't like the answer.

"Twelve hours," Torres said. He had checked the information before reporting to the fleet commander. "Assuming that we have to jump into a different vacant sector and travel to target at sub-light speeds. We can cut on time by jumping straight back in the *Tanto*, docking with the *Ichi* and all of us jumping out of the system."

"You're making a lot of assumptions for a one-hour safety window, Captain," Dassiova said.

Torres said nothing.

"Alright, put everything we have into getting the ships ready. Launch as soon as you have a green light."

CHAPTER 22

Deep Space Near Alpha Centauri

"Jump complete," the chief helmswoman of the *Norton* reported.

"Nothing on sensors," Torres said from the position he had taken at the tactical station.

Their mission had gone ahead with only four of them: two pilots and the two captains. It must have breached a dozen regulations, but the admiral had far bigger fish to fry than solving arguments over who got to go on what most would call a suicide mission.

"Shroud is holding," Torres told Halstead

She monitored the comm station where she helped input the navigational data. The other person on the mission, carrying the loneliest job of all of them, was Torres's chief pilot, sitting in the *Tanto*. The *Tanto* was docked to the nearest emergency airlock on their starboard side facing the stern. The emergency belly hatch of the small craft was open to the interior of the *Norton*, effectively part of its atmosphere until they sealed it and cut away.

The prototype shuttle belonging to the *Ichi* had also undergone rapid retrofitting of a Fold Drive and a shroud, neither of which had been granted more than basic testing before they were thrown into desperate service.

"Okay," Halstead said, her emotions at intentionally losing her ship dissipated in place of mission focus. "Two-thirds speed for six hours," she told her pilot.

"Picking up something on the sensors," Torres said. It seemed too short a time for the Va'alen to have responded to their jump signature from their base. "Single contact, energy signature matches the Va'alen... they're coming from the other direction, must've been close when we jumped in."

"Get us out of here, Lieutenant," Halstead said.

"We're outta here, ma'am," Lieutenant Cross answered. She pushed the fingers of her right hand up the power dial on her screen until the readout showed seventy percent.

"Not too fast," Torres warned. "She's a little bigger than the *Ichi* and we don't know what kind of wake we'll be leaving."

With a sigh, Cross dialed back the power to sixty-five percent and twitched her foot, making her right knee bounce into the helm console with an annoying repetition that Torres tried hard to ignore.

"Keep an eye on them, Torres," Halstead said.

"I am... they're static near our infil point now. Splitting off into pairs... two heading our way."

The temperature on the ghostly empty bridge of the big vessel seemed to drop about ten degrees as he waited for the next passive sweep to show the position of the enemy ships. The enemies that could tear them apart in a heartbeat. They only had power enough for half shields, even with their singularity power restored, and a single pair of gun turrets with minimal ammunition remaining. They had no hope of destroying more than the two ships heading in their direction, unless they were static at close range and totally unaware.

"Still following," Torres said. "Not gaining."

"We must be leaving a trace," Halstead said as she turned to another console and tapped at it furiously. She gasped slightly at what she read. "We're leaking atmosphere from deck four. There's not supposed to be any atmo on any decks but this one."

"Must have been a sealed compartment missed by the damage team. Can we vent it into another deck?" Cross asked.

"Trying," she replied tersely. "No. *Shit.* Environmental controls are shot. I can't do it from up here."

"Manual overrides?" Torres suggested.

"I'd have to get to deck four and override the safety protocols from the main control panel," Halstead said, rising from her seat.

She hit the control on her forearm comm device to activate her helmet and protect her from the vacuum; she was wearing the armor on Torres's insistence. She ran from the bridge, her voice coming back to them from the console speakers after she had left them.

"I'll have to airlock out after I've pumped the atmo to deck five," she said. "Keep an eye on those ships and tell me if they get inside weapons range or look like they've detected us."

"Aye, aye," Torres answered. "Be quick."

Halstead muttered something that didn't quite come through clearly, but the sentiment was obvious: she had no intention of stopping for a bite somewhere.

"Still not gaining," Torres reported. "They keep stopping and sending out active pings."

"How close?" Cross asked, her hand hovering over the main engine power output controls.

"Eighty thousand at last hit," he answered. "Their energy readings are… they're off the *chart!*"

"How so?" Halstead asked, her voice sounding muffled as she ran as fast as the confines of the ships ladders and decks would allow.

"It's nothing like our singularity drives," he said as he tried to interpret the readings. "Ours give off a pulse but these are… they're almost *humming*."

"Fascinating," Halstead said sarcastically. "Why are we only seeing this now?"

"They don't have their shields up and we've never gotten this close to them without being in a firefight."

"Great, so if they don't have any shields up, then why aren't we shooting them?"

Torres had to admit that was a good question.

"You want to go noisy this far from the objective?" Cross asked, reading his mind.

"If it's risk discovery this far out or risk being chased, I'd rather be chased," Halstead answered. "I'm at the control panel now, give me a minute."

"Fifty thousand," Torres reported. "They've accelerated."

"Any sign they've detected us?" Cross asked, her hand again ready to punch it to full power.

"No," he said. "They're in weapons range but haven't spun up their guns, from what I can tell."

"Forty-five seconds," Halstead said through clenched teeth.

She realized she had no tools to open the maintenance panel, then remembered that she was driving a powered armor suit. She dug the fingertips of her gauntlet into the joint and tore open the now-creased metal panel to expose the override controls. The seconds ticked by until the absent captain called for an update on the enemy position.

"They're grid-searching by the look of it," Torres said. "Still inside weapons range."

"We can't risk firing unless they're both static," Cross said unnecessarily.

Torres ignored her.

"Err, guys…" came another voice not yet heard on the channel. "I'm picking up another contact heading from the direction of the suns."

Rogers, strapped into the pilot seat of the *Tanto* with little to do but wait, saw the new sensor ping before Torres did, as the captain's attention was on the closest pair of enemy ships.

Torres looked at the readout and cursed. "Nicola, where are we with that atmo leak?"

"Ten seconds!"

Torres turned to Cross and gave her orders. "As soon as the leak is contained I want you to drop course thirty degrees and slow to fifty percent thrust."

She was professional enough not to question why and experienced enough to see the logic in his plan.

"Got it!" Halstead called. "Check it now?" Torres looked at the console she had vacated.

"You're good. Nice job. Get your ass back here." She acknowledged him.

"Captain?" Rogers asked again, reminding Torres that he hadn't answered his pilot.

"I hear you, Rogers," he said. "Stand by."

"Standing by," he mumbled back almost sarcastically. "Now, Cross," Torres hissed. She turned the nose of the frigate downward and slowed, holding her nerve in silence as Halstead walked back on the bridge and her helmet retracted to show her face.

"Did it work?" she asked, sliding back into the chair in front of the console.

"Hold on," Torres said, watching his own screen as he tracked the incoming ships converging from two sides. "They're holding at our last position… reading active sensor pings… their shields are up!"

"Plotting a jump course for the gateway device," Halstead snapped.

"Wait!" Torres said, holding out a hand to rest it on her right shoulder as he stared at the readout intently. "They're splitting off into a search pattern in pairs again."

Seconds ticked by in silence as they all waited, holding their breath to be sure that they were safe.

"Resume course, two-thirds power," Torres said quietly. Cross complied without speaking.

"Sit tight, Rogers," Torres said over the open comm.

"Panic over."

"Well that's a relief," he said. "I was just starting to wo—" An explosion shook the ship, vibrating them violently in their seats.

"Explosion on deck five," Halstead shouted. "Hull breach.

The air pressure from deck four must have screwed something. All the atmo has vented… reading electrical failures there."

"Anything vital?" Cross asked, worried that she might lose power to her engines or maneuvering thrusters.

"No, but the power spikes will be visible now that we have a hull breach." She turned to Torres, fearing what she knew he was about to say.

"Four incoming. Weapons are hot," he said in a hollow voice. "Make the jump."

Halstead turned to Cross. The pilot didn't hesitate.

They emerged from the jump and immediately the sounds of klaxons filled the bridge.

"Too close to the sun!" Cross called out, hitting an emergency button to make two joysticks emerge from the arms of her chair.

She grabbed the manual controls and hauled on them, her feet hitting the pedals that had come up from the deck. She pushed them to full power, trying to escape the gravity well of the massive star before it sucked them too close and fried them a thousand miles away from the surface of the burning orb. The ship vibrated terribly, making them grab on as the external forces threatened to overpower the ship's grav emitter.

"What the hell is going on?" Rogers shouted from his blind position strapped in at the controls of their getaway ride.

"No time," Torres growled. "Stand by."

"Get us out of here, Charlotte, *now!*" Halstead yelled at Cross. Using her given name for the first time only served to underline the desperation of their situation.

"Trying!" The pilot growled through gritted teeth as she hauled on the controls with all her strength.

"Diverting all auxiliary power to the port thrusters," Torres said.

"No! Main engines!" Cross yelled.

Torres diverted the power again unquestioningly, not bothering to argue with an officer who evidently knew her trade better than he did. He was sure if they ever found themselves in a covert terrorist takedown, then both of them would follow his lead, but out there in the void, with a battered ship and enemy converging, he shut his mouth and did as he was told.

"We're locked, goddammit," Cross shouted. "I can't break us free!"

"Jump us!" Halstead shouted.

215

"From a gravity well?" Torres yelled over the sound of the awful vibration that would surely tear the ship apart. The full power of the engines was trapped in a battle against the power of the sun's gravity like a free faller hitting terminal velocity.

"Tenth of a second straight ahead," the *Norton's* captain shouted. "One tenth of a second. Ready?"

"Do it!" Cross said with difficulty, a vein pulsing visibly on her right temple as she fought the controls.

Halstead hit the jump activation icon on her console, making them all fall forward when the pressure on their bodies suddenly disappeared. They sat in sudden silence caused by the absence of vibration. Torres looked at his readout as the display reset to a different part of the sector.

"Target is four hundred thousand klicks away." He gave Cross a bearing and she turned the ship before sending it towards the gateway at full power.

"Time to target?" Halstead called out, her voice loud still despite the lack of noisy vibration.

"Six minutes, ready the detonation sequence," Torres said.

He called his own pilot over the open channel. "Rogers, you still with us?"

"What the hell was that?" the man yelled back. His was voice a full two octaves higher as though the atmosphere on the *Tanto* had suddenly increased its helium content to match the carbon dioxide.

"Just the gravity of Alpha Centauri. You all good?" Torres answered.

"You mean the gravity well of a star bigger than our sun? Well, no wonder I'm blind!"

"Rogers, focus up!" Torres said. "Are you good?"

"I'm, *we're*, in one piece, sir."

"Good, get your ass ready for the best flying you've ever done because you'll need to get us clear under some less than ideal circumstances."

"You mean the circumstances where I've got about... *nine* incoming enemy signatures?"

"Yeah," Torres told him, mentally multiplying nine by four and not liking the number he came up with.

"Oh, okay," Rogers quipped back. "So... no in-flight movie?"

"Your guy always such a kid, sir?" Cross asked from the helm.

"I think he's got ADD or something," Torres said. "But he's a damned good pilot."

Over the comm they heard Rogers huff and Cross snort derision at the threat to her piloting supremacy.

"Approaching target," Torres said. "Readying detonation timer."

"Oh, hell this is going to be tight," Halstead muttered.

Unseen by any of them, Rogers bit down an inappropriate joke that he knew came to his lips as a by-product of intense stress.

"One minute," Cross said.

"Enemy contacts on intercept course, multiple targets," Torres responded. "Ninety seconds. Rogers?" he shouted, barely breathing between subjects as he hailed the *Tanto*'s pilot.

"Go," he snapped back.

"Nothing to lose now," Torres said quickly. "Run as many active sensor pings as you can and record the data for if we get out of here."

Rogers didn't acknowledge, but Torres new he'd be doing it already. It wasn't as though stealth was an issue by that point.

"Cuttin' it fine, man," Halstead mumbled, drawing the words out. She had intended to speak to herself but forgot the open comm link active between their suits.

"Approaching the gateway device now," Cross said. "Brace for emergency reverse thrust in three... two... one..."

They braced, feeling the extreme forces of inertia beating the power of the ship's emitter for a heartbeat. They all held their breath to prevent their lungs from collapsing and driving the air out of their chests.

"Where do I park it?" Cross asked.

"Anywhere," Halstead shot back. "Just put her as close to the ring as possible and set the auto-pilot."

Cross did, hitting the icon to activate the pre-programmed sequence that would maneuver the frigate to rest alongside the device.

"Go!" Torres shouted. "Get to the *Tanto*."

They ran, Halstead pausing in the open doorway of her bridge to look back one last time, only to see Torres still at the tactical station.

"Come on, Kyle!" she shouted. "Move it, Torres!"

"I'm engaging the closest ships," he yelled back. "The auto guns can't target their movements effectively."

"It doesn't matter," the other captain yelled back. "We need to go, *now!*"

"Arrgh!" Torres abandoned the tactical station with a frustrated growl as he thumped an impotent fist onto the glass and turned away. His gauntlets and helmet activated to wrap him in the pressurized armor ready to run and jump in their ride like they'd just robbed the mother of all banks.

"I hope you're ready, Rogers," he said, flicking his eyes over the HUD controls to hit the start button on the detonation countdown, "because in forty seconds part of this sector is going to be one big collapsing singularity."

"Err, waitin' on you, boss."

"I know," Torres yelled. He pulled himself up through the emergency airlock hatch and into the belly of their ship.

He rolled as he got inside, glancing up to see Charlotte Cross strapping herself in beside Rogers and Halstead hitting the emergency hatch closure icon on the terminal built into the bulkhead of the ship.

"We're sealed," she shouted as she threw herself into the nearest seat and racked on her straps. Torres did the same opposite her. "Punch it!"

"Go," Torres shouted at the same time.

Rogers went. He had kept their little ship shrouded the entire time in the vain hope that the enemy wouldn't detect a piece of the alien ship breaking away and taking off like a cat with its ass on fire.

The forces of the ship's acceleration would have killed them had they not been in powered armor that responded to the physics in play. Still, the air was driven from their lungs making talking impossible. It even made it seem as though the ship had no gravity emitter.

"Hold on," Rogers said.

The others recognized in his tone the stupid way that pilots and drivers always spoke when they were about to do something that good sense and self-preservation told them that they shouldn't; like a blind overtake toward the brow of a hill on a bend or running a gauntlet of far superior enemy ships outnumbering them about forty to one. All they could do was hold on tight and wait. They would either die in an instant or make it out, and only one of them had any chance of affecting that outcome.

"Whoa," Rogers yelled. "Son of a bi—"

"What the hell, man?" Cross shouted.

"Sorry," Rogers said. "Li'l bastard came outta nowhere…" They could do nothing but wait; their fate in the hands of someone else, and no matter how good he was or how good anyone else *said* he was, they were still powerless to affect their situation.

The hull vibrated as concussive waves pounded them.

"Moving too fast for the shroud to be effective!" Rogers yelled. "Drop it and divert that power to the shields."

Cross hit the buttons to make it happen. Three more heavy thumps rocked the ship as Rogers threw it through space like he'd just stolen it.

"Shields to sixty percent!" Cross hollered. "You *aiming* to get hit?"

"Tray tables in the upright position…" Rogers responded in a grumble, his face glued to the readouts and his hands working the controls like a man possessed. "We're clear, hit that jump sequence. It's preloaded ready."

"Hold on," Torres shouted. "Don't jump until we know the gateway is toast."

"How long?" Rogers bawled back. He was so loud, their suits automatically dampened the volume of their speakers to protect their hearing.

"Fourteen seconds," Halstead called out. Having had little to do, she had been watching the countdown on her HUD to block out the stress of their escape.

Those fourteen seconds felt like a lifetime. The enemy ships had all but abandoned the pursuit of them in favor of pouring fire into the frigate at close range since it appeared to be trying to dock with the gateway.

"Three, two, one," Halstead said. "See ya, fuc—"

The explosion from the gateway, magnified by the singularity energy sources and almost every spare warhead from the fleet packed into the *Norton*'s empty cargo holds, rocked them in their seats.

"Is it gone?" Torres asked.

"Is *what* gone?" Cross answered. "I can't even see any parts left."

"Get us out of here, Rogers," Torres ordered. "*Punch it.*"

CHAPTER 23

Deep Space Near Proxima Centauri

"Jump signature detected," cried the tactical officer on the bridge of the *Ichi*.

Brandt winced, annoyed at the noise but more annoyed with herself for jumping out of her skin at the suddenness of it.

"Thank you, Ensign," she growled. "Any more information or am I to guess?"

"It's the *Tanto*, Commander," he said in a voice far less excitable.

"Incoming hail, ma'am," the comm officer reported. "Audio only."

"On screen," Brandt answered. She cursed herself for speaking the command automatically but was grateful that the comm officer knew what she meant. He activated the speaker. Brandt breathed out, settling her butt back into the chair she didn't quite feel ready to be driving. Torres's voice reverberated around the bridge, too loud for the confined space.

"*Ichi, Tanto,* come in."

"We're here, Captain," Brandt answered. "Mission report?"

"All good, get the docking bay doors open and prepare to jump as soon as we're sealed. Torres out."

Brandt closed her mouth to stifle the words she had loaded ready to respond, hoping that none of the junior officers saw her nervousness.

"Tactical. Helm," she said. "You heard the captain. Get ready."

Hurtling through the empty void as fast as possible in their small ship, Torres tried to ignore the verbal warning from Cross sitting up front to report the incoming wave of enemy ships visible on her sensors. Torres used the visual controls of his suit's HUD to activate the comm channel to the fleet's flagship. His priority had been getting his ride out of there before he gave the good news. The hail was answered in under a second. He guessed they were doing little else, other than waiting for his call.

"Torres, this is the admiral," the voice in his ear said. "Give me good news."

"Gateway device destroyed, sir," Torres said. He paused as he heard a muted cheer come from the other end of the open link.

"Get your ass aboard your ship, Captain," Dassiova told him. "The fleet is going to jump one light year away and reconvene; I don't want anyone getting separated at the closing stages."

"Understood, sir."

"And Captain?" Dassiova asked.

"Sir?"

"Good job. To all of you. I look forward to hearing the whole story very soon. *Venture* out."

Dassiova had one last job to do, one last mission parameter to fulfill, before he jumped the damaged remains of the brand-new fleet back to their own system. Giving the orders to his tactical station, the sequence of commands was inputted and the launch bay doors on the port side to their stern slid silently open.

The firing sequence was programmed to activate in the seconds before their choreographed jump signatures sent out a flare to every sensor in the sector. It was designed to carry the hastily built subspace sensor array far from their last known coordinates. This would disguise it among the small pieces of debris locked into the orbit of the curious half-frozen planet hurtling around the red dwarf.

That array, like a hidden buoy in dark waters, possessed an almost endless energy source that powered the passive sensors, the shroud device—tiny in comparison to those installed on the ships—and the small subspace communication array that sent back a pulse of data every twelve hours.

That hidden, mechanical spy would be their eyes and ears until they could re-arm, re-fit and return with more ships. Faster and stronger ships. Better armed ships. Ships to take control of the entire system and more than double the power of Earth.

Their return, if successful, would mark the beginning of the Earth empire.

The *Tanto*, a tiny speck against the vastness of the two colony ships, slid to what appeared to be a graceful arrest of momentum. The nose turned to align perfectly for sliding into the docking bay of its big sister, the *Ichi*. They had tried to get the Kuldar's one ship to dock with them, but the rounded, smooth lines of the ship made it too tight to fit, so it went into a hangar bay onboard the *Venture*.

The three remaining ships—one small and agile-looking, one large with another docked to its belly and one gargantuan —seemed so still and at peace in the soft, red glow coming from the nearby star.

Further away from them, at a distance that would mean days of travel on the surface of any planet but in the empty void would take mere minutes to traverse, the dusting of shiny stars seemed to ripple. A huge wave of distortion approached the resting ships with an ominous air of dread about it. The distortion rippled more intensely, breaking apart and seeming to stretch the imaginary covering of invisibility like it was a thin sheet of plastic, straining until, as one, the two flanks broke away and shimmered into solid ships that split off in pairs. The entire approaching armada, dispatched at their maximum sub-light speed as soon as they received first reports of an alien invasion, spread out into an attacking line. They charged shields and powered up their weapons. Almost fifty ships, uncountable with any accuracy by Torres's happenstance discovery of them, faced the three vessels of differing size. They were as yet totally unaware that they would be returning to their hub to find devastation. They could not predict the terrifying news of being cut off from their own system by the destruction of the gateway device.

As the order rippled along the many pairs of Va'alen fighter ships, their three targets blinked into nothingness; vanishing from the galaxy in the blink of a human eye.

Confusion reigned. The next five days were spent in desperate search of the aliens all over the sector before the order came for them to swarm again and begin the long journey home. During that time, believing themselves totally alone in that part of the system, their communications often went unencrypted. As such, they were picked up by the passive sensor left behind as it hid in a tiny patch of nothingness and pretended not to exist. Those communications, along with the detailed scans of the ships and the recording of their search movements, was sent back over the four-and-one-third light years via the tiny subspace worm hole created by the comm relay to be analyzed by the humans.

Deep Space, Just Outside the Oort Cloud of Earth's Solar System

"Jump complete," the pilot of the *Cortez* reported.

"Thank you, Mister Moon," Captain Wright answered, his British accent sounding oddly at home commanding the bridge crew of a large vessel. Their third short jump since leaving the system to journey home had taken them to just outside their home system. It sparked the repeat of shortening the distances between the three ships as their Fold Drive exit locations still varied too much for their liking.

"Tactical, have you located the other fleet ships?" he asked, turning his head slightly.

"I have the *Ichi* nine thousand kilometers to our stern— looks like we overshot them—and the *Venture...*" He trailed off as he zoomed out to enlarge the sector of space they currently inhabited.

"The *Venture*?" Wright prompted. He heard nothing in reply and held his tongue for as long as he thought befitted the rank above his own. He could not, however, wait so long that it seemed as though he tolerated being ignored. "Tactical?"

"Sorry, sir... I'm... I'm picking something up now... *Got her!* Sir, the *Venture* is six thousand kilometers to our starboard side."

"Very good," Wright said, hiding his fleeting moment of dismay that the admiral's flagship was not lost. That would have left him in command and providing the report to Earth personally.

He had no way of knowing that the subspace comm blackout was an order from Dassiova, passed on by Earth. He also wasn't aware their destination was not Earth after all but was the now repurposed Mars base.

A lot had happened on Earth in their short absence, though arguably not as much as had in the Centauri system.

"Hail from the *Venture,* Captain," his comm officer called out.

"On screen," he said. Wright settled back in his chair to try and look magisterial as he put on a smile of smug competence ready to face Dassiova.

"Negative, sir, data only. Orders to re-route to Mars orbit; distance of twenty thousand kilometers out and proceed at sub-light speed."

Wright frowned, his next words showing just how far ahead he liked to think.

"Has the admiral thought to order the fleet to jump into the Red Run path to make it look as though we came from where we were supposed to?" he asked, raising an eyebrow at his comm officer.

She turned and relayed the question with far more tact and less of a passive-aggressive tone than her captain had used.

"Negative, sir, the admiral says…" She faltered, hesitating before reading out the words.

"The admiral says what, precisely?" Wright needled her.

She could have sent the message directly to his console beside the captain's chair, but the way he spoke down to her and their proximity to home made her brave enough to get the smallest amount of revenge on the man everyone on the bridge rotation was beginning to dislike.

"The admiral," she said confidently, "sends his compliments, and asks that the captain follows orders and stops second-guessing him, unless he desires a size eleven boot-enema, sir."

Wright gave a small and unconvincing laugh, trying to pass off the harsh words from Dassiova as mere captain-to-captain bantering. They all knew it wasn't; if they found him irritating, then there was no doubt that the admiral would have likely meant every word he said.

"The admiral requests a personal response, Captain," the comm officer went on, trying not to enjoy the humiliation of the man in front of his crew.

Wright gave another false chuckle and tapped at the console beside him, typing out a brief acknowledgment of both the orders and the reminder to follow orders.

He knew how to fake humility when it was required, and he also knew how to use the politicians to his advantage. His own report, submitted independently of the *Cortez*'s logs, would indicate his opinion that Earth made a mistake in putting an attack dog in charge of a fleet. This opinion was supported by their heavy losses of both personnel and resources—especially the intentional destruction of a newly refitted frigate. His approach appealed to the politicians holding the purse strings, as so often that dictated policy more than any moral objective.

They set the jump coordinates, felt that familiar sensation of momentary weightlessness, and ran an active sensor sweep to find a very different set of circumstances at the planet than when they had last seen Mars.

CHAPTER 24

Approaching Mars Orbit

"Incoming hail, Admiral," the comm officer said. "Mars shipyards CO requesting we squawk ident and transmit authority codes. Do we even have shipyards on Mars...?"

"Acknowledged," Dassiova said, ignoring her question and typing in his personal UNID authorization code.

This should act as an access-all-areas backstage pass and scare the hell out of any deep space commander with an idea of challenging his authority. To his surprise, a similar set of codes was transmitted back, giving a clearance level almost the same as his own.

"Open a channel," the admiral ordered, eager to find out who the person was on the other end. "On screen."

"Admiral Dassiova," the confident man on the screen said as he cracked into a genuine half-smile. "I am Commander Novak, European Territory UNID. Pleasure to make your acquaintances." The accent was curious; Russian in rhythm and syntax but somehow Americanized in the occasional pronunciation as though most of his English had been learned by watching movies.

"Commander," Dassiova answered gruffly, "care to fill me in on the new developments there?"

"Of course," Novak answered with a smile. "The entire planetary base was taken over by our combined territories UNID and special

229

operations group shortly after you left the solar system. We have the new shipyards and equipment production in full flow both in the orbitings and down here on the surfaces.

"All non-UNID and Hyper personnel have been evacuated due to a contaminant leak here—"

"What contaminant?" Dassiova interrupted.

"Oh, there's no contaminant, Admiral. This is merely the cover story we used for, how you say, the *mushrooms*?" Novak said, still smiling.

"So, this is, what?" Dassiova growled. "Our staging area?"

"That is a good way to say this. If you wouldn't mind docking at platform number nine, I will have dropships sent to escort your senior officers to the surface first. There are R&R stations set up down here for your crew but all of this in good time. I'm unlocking the communications blackout now, but I must insist that your ships disable their comm links to Earth via both normal and sub space methods. Sorry, orders from the man."

Dassiova understood, expecting it, but was at least relieved to know that they wouldn't be cold-quarantined in some dull base back in Earth orbit to prevent the word getting out.

"Understood, Commander," Dassiova said. "Be with you shortly. *Venture* out."

The *Venture* docked at platform nine on the lowest level of the big, skeletal space station opposite a half-built vessel of the same size. That vessel looked modular, as though the hull was intentionally incomplete, and the *Cortez* was ordered into position on the top-most level.

Tug ships swooped in to assist the *Hammer* in releasing her docking clamps and limping to a dry dock of her own. Support arms moved to surround the battered frigate before the shielding activated and the artificial atmosphere was pumped in to allow the ship to be worked on without a spacewalk being required every time the exterior needed attention.

As per their orders, the senior officers of each ship congregated at the airlock where a heavy dropship, also retrofitted with a Fold Drive, took them to the Mars surface. For those of the *Ichi*, this was the last place they had been in their own solar system before their jump to Centauri, and that visit had been less than comfortable. The dropship ride was less bumpy than the elevator on the shipyard station, and their ride to the surface was brief.

Dassiova took his flight officer, Suranne Massey—the brusque woman who ran the ship efficiently, but who he never really got along with on a personal level—and the commander of his ground troops. He fully intended to replace one of those people for the return trip, and he didn't put much importance on personal relationships. He had a far better man in mind to lead his ground-pounders on the next mission in the Centauri system. Captains Hayes and Halstead each came alone. Their ships were not large enough to be equipped with a detachment of UNPF ground troops, nor did frigates operate with the flight officer position. Captain Wright, bustling along, brought his flight officer—a man who looked more than ready to be stood down—and an ageing commander of their troop detachment who also seemed eager to be away from the ship.

Torres brought Brandt and the tall Scandinavian flight officer who seemed decent at his job.

Dassiova had to admit that his old ensign and junior NCO had done well, along with the two others who had been under his command. He had limited the number of officers in the briefing to the most senior of the ships, even the now-destroyed frigate, to minimize the amount of time they would be stuck with the inevitable round of questions when the briefing ended.

Dassiova felt that was one of the small curses to plague his life. He had felt this way since he first arrived for his induction briefing at the officer candidate school in Rhode Island. Even then, over two and half decades before, when the young man about to be inducted into the ranks of fresh ensigns in the UNPF, he had been greatly anticipating lunch and trying to make himself as still as possible whenever his stomach growled, and furtive glances came his way. His memories of that lunch, delayed a full fifteen minutes by the questions being asked by too many people being crammed into one room, still haunted him to that day.

"Admiral?" Wright asked, eyebrows up and waiting for an answer.

Dassiova shook his head, shaken from his exhaustion caused by having been at sea under intense stress for too long.

"Captain?" he asked, annoyed that the other man refused to call him 'Sir' and be done with it. He always insisted on using his rank.

"I asked if you knew how long we would be held here, or whether we will be sent on to Earth any time soon?"

"Well, if you listen to the briefing we're about to get I imagine we'll all learn something," Dassiova grumbled at Wright. This exchange let everyone know his opinion about premature and stupid questions. They walked down the ramp of the dropship, through a hangar airlock and into the warm greeting of Commander Novak.

"Welcome, Admiral," he said, shaking the man's hand despite his thinly veiled fury at being touched. The commander insisted on shaking the hand of every one of the group arriving at his command. "Please, come, it is great honors to have you here. You are all great hero of Earth!" He beamed at them, lapsing them all into an embarrassed silence.

"Commander," Dassiova said carefully, "we've had a bit of a long ride… you have a briefing docket for us?"

"Yes," Novak said, jumping to action and striding ahead toward the doors marked as the briefing room. They followed, filtering around the large table in the wide room where most of them couldn't help but notice the stitched lines of bullet holes in one wall.

"Commander?" Torres said, unable to keep silent given the signs of recent conflict. "What happened here?"

"There was some…err how you say, *resistances*? To our evacuation…"

"So, we've taken Mars by force and are holding it illegally?" Torres asked, feeling unable to contain himself given the possibility that their actions had caused more loss of life than they had already inflicted on the enemy in the distant Centauri System.

"No, not this," Novak said. "Please, sit and I will activate the comm link."

They sat, not wasting any more breath asking questions of a man who probably wasn't at liberty to answer them. Novak waited for a pair of seamen to enter bearing trays of coffee pots and cups before shutting the doors and swiping the controls with his right arm. The door clicked shut and the light above it went from green to red. He tapped at the console and the large display wall flickered to life.

"Mars base briefing room with senior officers from the Ninth Fleet," Novak said. "Room is secure."

"Admiral. Officers," said the voice on the other end. The camera moved and the face of a suited man and an unfamiliar admiral came into view. "I'll keep this brief and fill you in on the events since the fleet left the system."

"Sir," Dassiova barked in interruption, "your name and position for the record?"

The fact that he had voiced what most of them were already thinking didn't soften the mood at all. The suited man looked at the admiral beside him, a much older man with an air of impatience, and wore a look of incredulity at being addressed as he had been. The admiral shrugged as if to say that he wore a uniform, but the suited man could have been anyone.

"Admiral Dassiova, my name is Chase Ettington. I am the director of the American Territory UNID. Does that satisfy?"

"It does, sir," Dassiova said without flinching or missing a beat. "Please, continue."

"As I was saying," Ettington went on, his annoyance at being interrupted gone, "since the fleet left Earth there have been some... *developments*."

None of the officers seated around the table responded, thinking it better to wait.

"I'll be frank, we came very close to a large-scale conflict and a lot of political work has gone on behind the scenes to keep this from happening. As it stands, currently the territory of Africa and a good deal of what used to be the Middle East is standing against America, Europe and Asia. Russia and Australasia were standing independently but have now got onboard with us. It's just a numbers game, and unless the separatists can convince another territory to ally with them then there won't be another war.

"That said, almost everywhere is on high alert for terror attacks and we have had to create probably our biggest cover-up for what transpired on the lunar surface." His eyes lingered on Brandt and

Torres. The *Ichi*'s current, and likely very soon to become *former* captain shifted in his chair and cleared his throat.

"Save it, Commander," Ettington said. "No blame will land at your or your team's feet over this. We all have far bigger fish to fry. Speaking of which…" He paused, glancing again at the admiral who cleared his own throat and spoke.

"The construction of the new additions to the Ninth Fleet are underway," he said. "We are constructing some of the ships at the Mars station since their configuration would raise more than a few questions from the civilian population. What you'll have eventually, which is subject to change of course, is the following…" He listed the ships now assigned to or being built especially for the fleet. Those ships would require over double the personnel that they already had, or had set off with before they met the Va'alen. The intelligence and other data sent back made the abandonment of the system unthinkable for their task masters.

When he had finished, the eyes of the senior officers in the room grew wide and stayed there. What the admiral had just promised them was twice the size and strength of any force ever amassed in the history of the UNPF. It was Dassiova's turn to clear his throat.

"And personnel, sir?" he asked hopefully.

"Unless there are any members of your crews which you need to replace, the current assigned troops will remain. Their official tour lasts for another sixteen months, which we anticipate would be more than long enough the get the job done, and other resources assigned to you will also be on long-term deployment."

"And our orders, sir?"

"Your orders are simple," Ettington told him. "We give you a bigger fleet, you use the time it takes to build it and get it to you to train and strategize, then you go back to the Centauri system and remove all hostile elements for a full-scale colonization plan. Understood?"

"Aye, aye," Dassiova growled. "What about our new friends we have on our ships?"

"Commander Novak has more details on that," Ettington said, "but they will be housed in temporary shelters on Mars designed for their individual needs. When they've given up their technical knowledge and we can learn nothing new then we will dispatch a mission to take them to a world habitable for them. They keep their word and we shall keep ours—it's that simple."

CHAPTER 25

Mars Orbit Shipyard

Seven Months Later

"I've been saving this for a special occasion," Dassiova said. He hosted the three other fleet captains who had accepted his invitation. He poured four glasses, careful not to spill a drop of the precious liquid, and handed one each to Halstead,

Hayes and Torres.

"Congratulations on making the cut," he told them, raising his glass as they mirrored his gesture. They murmured their own sentiments and the four senior officers settled down to as close a state of relaxation as was possible when being hosted by your fleet admiral. "I may as well tell you now, Captain Wright has written a separate report about our activities in the Centauri system, and has been damning of all of us. Apparently, we are reckless, egotistical and arrogant with, what he describes as, 'God complexes'."

"I assume he's on a slow boat back to Earth?" Hayes asked with a smirk.

Dassiova saw his smirk and raised him an evil smile.

"No, he's still the captain of the *Cortez*, and I blocked his application to be rotated out of the fleet."

Their expressions asked why, even if their mouths stayed silent.

"The *Cortez* will be fitted out as a resup vessel only. She's our store cupboard and won't take part in any action. She won't get a gun upgrade, but she will get better shields. It means that your frigates will carry minimal supplies to make way for your extra guns and warheads, so you'll dock with the food boat more often. I'm sure he'll invite you aboard to dine with him…"

Both Hayes and Halstead smiled at that, no doubt anticipating the annoyance of the man that tried to destroy their careers. The two captains were also in gleeful anticipation at getting their gunships back.

Those frigates—one new and one painstakingly rebuilt—were the big hitters of Dassiova's new fleet. They were so overpowered and over-gunned that their use in their home system was a concern to everyone. Nothing that powerful could go unopposed, so the alliance between the friendly territories had allowed for full disclosure and sharing of new technology. The idea was to force the rogue nations to accept the way of things and fall peacefully into line.

"And your new ship, Admiral?" Torres asked. He was overjoyed to be retaining the *Ichi* with her original crew and minus the refugees.

Dassiova smiled; a rare sight under any circumstances.

"The *Indomitable* will be getting a few design tweaks," he said as he cast a look around the grand captain's quarters onboard the *Venture*. He would soon be departing his old ship. That new flagship, a carrier that was more of a huge gunship with eight sections missing where the agile and well-armed destroyers were locked in, was nearing readiness. The eight missing parts of her whole were travelling from Earth where they had been built. They looked like innocuous-enough standard destroyers traveling towards them at sub-light speed.

"And who gets the *Venture*?" Hayes asked.

"You'll find out when you find out," Dassiova said, guessing correctly that the scuttlebutt had already reached their ears. In his book, any senior officer who didn't listen to the gossip of the men and women under their command didn't deserve a command at all.

Still, he reminded himself, *listening to it and believing it are two different things.*

"The parts are all but assembled," Halstead spoke up. She had heard this directly from the shipyard teams who had been working tirelessly for over half a year to get them ready to put to sea again. "It's just a matter of fitting it together so that the Centauri system station activates properly."

That was a later addition to their plan, hence the current delay. The choice to drop a permanent station in the system was a sound one met with unanimous agreement.

"And our little green friends?" Dassiova asked Torres. The admiral knew that he out all of them spent the most time on the dome-covered surface of Mars with the Hyper and UN science teams, developing the new weapons that were hastily being manufactured for fitting to the ships.

Given their previous experience having their asses handed to them by a handful of small alien ships, they had adopted the old mantra of two being better than one. Where there had once been a big quad-barreled chain gun, there now stood a pair of the new ship-mounted bolt cannons.

These guns, simply massive upscaled versions of their new personal weapons, made the concept of protection on Earth an irrelevance. It was a good thing they were on lockdown, because the technology even one of their ships possessed was likely to rival every traditional weapon they had back on Earth. The only way to make everyone there safe again was to share the technology, both offensive and defensive.

"Still working hard," Torres answered with a smile. "The single Va'alen arm that my team managed to shoot off and bring back has been invaluable to research."

"I heard about this," Halstead said, sitting forward. "Is it true it's made of a natural kind of Kevlar or something?"

"Overlapping layers of bio-mesh that acts like a kind of armor, yes," Torres said, repeating what he had been told. He had asked Paterson to dumb it down for him. "It also continues to heal, even though it's been in the freezer for so long. The parts of it used for weapons testing didn't exactly regenerate though, put it that way."

"And our, err, *enhanced*, crewmember?" Dassiova asked. He had taken more of an interest in Specter since remembering the carnage he had faced in that terrorist attack.

"He was under for quite a bit of the time," Torres answered, "until a team from Hyper made the jump out here. They've fixed him up, corrected the damage, or so they think, then put their people to work on the alien tech. I think it's fair to say they'll have some nice improvements for us if we have to slug it out toe-to-toe with the cockroaches again." He winced inside at his use of the popular derogatory nickname for their enemy, but nobody seemed to notice.

"I look forward to it," Dassiova said with a smile and drained his glass.

He didn't move to refill it, and the others took that as their sign to dismiss themselves. They made their goodbyes and went back to their respective ships; Halstead to her temporary quarters on the *Venture* until her new command was ready and Torres and Hayes to their own ships.

Dassiova sat alone with the lights turned down low as he finished the expensive bottle of brandy he had been carrying for a long time. He sat staring out of one of the few portholes on the vast ship, one of the perks of command. It was like his private picture window. He stayed in silent thought for a long time as he drank. Halfway through his fourth glass he let out a small gasp of a sob which he quickly stifled, clearing his throat angrily as though he could remove the lump of emotion with sheer willpower alone. He cuffed at the tear that rolled gently down the pitted and weathered skin of his right cheek.

The special occasion he had been saving the bottle for was not a happy one, despite his invitations to the captains who had earned his trust. He merely wanted to share the bottle with other people so that he didn't drink the whole thing alone.

His father had bought it during one of his more lucid periods, and had it shipped to his son before he set off for who-knew-where on the mission he wouldn't talk about. He sent a note with the bottle that simply read, "Bring this back and we can drink it together. Carry it with you so you know how proud I am, even if I forget to say so."

He had received the communiqué on Mars via standard comm traffic from Earth. The comm simply informed the admiral that as of the date exactly thirty-one days prior, his father had passed away in the early hours after suffering a stroke. The note assured the admiral that his father did not suffer, but it said nothing about him dying in the company of another human being to offer the warmth of companionship.

He swallowed the last of the drink, feeling it sour in his stomach before replacing the glass to the table and heading for his rack. Unencumbered by an attachment to anyone left on Earth, Elias

Dassiova fell asleep knowing that his home, now and until he died, or they forced him to retire, was the Ninth Fleet.

And it was going to war.

EPILOGUE

Orbit of Alpha Centauri

The Va'alen supreme commander watched through a clear forcefield as the maintenance team below retrieved the artifact. It had taken them days to reconstruct the explosion from their sensors and create a replay of what had happened. When the nose of the ship that had destroyed their only way home was seen blasted out ahead of the singularity crushing the exploded wreckage into nothingness, the race was on to project its trajectory and catch up to retrieve it.

Now, after months of his ships pushing their engines hard to find and seize it, the supreme commander was looking down as the hull was cut away to reveal what appeared to be a new kind of power source. It was a new type of field generator and, most curiously of all, a strange device with a long spike that jutted out ahead of the fuselage.

He turned and hissed his orders to the entourage that followed the supreme commander everywhere he went. He wasn't known to be patient when he desired something.

"Tell the engineers I want to know what that does and how it works," he said as he pointed the two hands of his left side at the spiked contraption, "and if it is their way to make the invisible gateways then I want one fitted to all of our ships."

The entourage bowed deeply as he waved them away, all of them smaller and physically feebler than his grand armor made him. He turned, activated a holo-display with his lower set of clawed hands as his uppers simultaneously cupped the part of his blank face where a chin would be and leaned his weight against the wall.

The message played on a loop, showing endless pictures of the human home world and their history. It gave stellar charts, and the supreme commander could not understand why an enemy so formidable—if weak in body and weaponry—would hand over a map to their world so that anyone could find it. The pictures and data transmitted by the first ship to appear as if it came through a gateway also gave complex and detailed anatomical intelligence, which made it easier to kill them. The Va'alen, a word in Kuldar which translated as Demon, but in their own tongue literally read as Combatant, were only the tip of the iceberg as far as the problems for humans were concerned. Their multi-species alliance was vast, impossibly strong, and when the Va'alen found a way to reconnect with the rest of their swarms, then the humans and the filthy, treacherous Kuldar they had rescued would all die.

But first, the supreme commander thought, *we must find a way out of this system before we perish.*

END OF BOOK TWO

Remember to sign up for my emailing list at **www. devoncford.com**
Follow me on social media for cover reveals, release information and general shenanigans:

Facebook: @devoncfordofficial

Instagram: @dcf_actual

Also by Devon C Ford

The *After It Happened* series:
(Also on Audible)

1 – Survival (Performed by R.C Bray)

2 – Humanity (Performed by R.C Bray)

3 – Society (Performed by R.C Bray)

4 – Hope (Performed by R.C Bray)

5 – Sanctuary (Performed by R.C Bray)

6 – Rebellion (Performed by R.C Bray)

7 – Andorra (The Leah Chronicles, performed by Kate Reading)

8 – Piracy (The Leah Chronicles, performed by Kate Reading)

9 – Home (Performed by R.C Bray)

The *New Earth* series:
(Also on Audible Performed by Marc Vietor)

1 – ARC

2 - SWARM (with Chris Harris)

The *Burning Skies* Multi-Author series:
(Also on Audible read by Neil Hellegers)

1 – The Fall

2 – Fallout (by Jacqueline Druga)

3 – Uprising (by Chris Harris)